Still A Rose

Lisa Webb Timley

ISBN 978-0-6151-8808-9

*Published by CreativeWorkz Publishing, a division
of CreativeSportz
Jacksonville, FL 32225*

For Leila and Gabby, the loves of my life.

Disclaimer

This is a work of fiction. Any similarities to any person, living or dead, is purely coincidental.

Table of Contents

8

New Beginnings

Moving to Jacksonville was a good move for me. Nice weather, decent people. I pretty much like it here, aside from all the road construction and daily detours. It's a welcome change from drama-filled Atlanta. I must admit I'm a down home Georgia girl, but I had my share of DRAMA in Atlanta. Friends turned foes, lovers turned enemies, and I could NOT take another day of that damn traffic. Yep, Florida was definitely the right way to go.

I settled in for my nightly ritual while listening to Katie Couric tell me that unemployment is at an all time high. Katie hasn't been the same since leaving the Today Show. Without Matt Lauer she is just another boring face in the crowd. After changing the channel, I rubbed Vaseline Intensive care-well actually the two dollar Equate brand from Wal-mart that works just as well, on every inch of skin I could reach. My body is not in the shape it used to be in. I stand 5'6 and weigh in at 180 pounds. Everybody tells me I carry it well and am well proportioned, but I long to be thin again. Despite the extra curvy rolls, I put lotion everywhere to keep my skin supple. I don't care how big I get, I refuse to get stretch marks. A little FDS to keep things cool, fresh, and feminine, and I am ready for bed. I put on my long cotton pajamas even though it is June in Florida-Hot. I put them on partly because I don't feel like looking at myself in anything shorter.

I plop down on the floor and grab my cell phone to check for missed calls. None. I thought

Sean would have called because I told him I have something important to tell him. I don't, but I wanted him to call. Not the case. Sean is the typical NBA player. He eats, sleeps, and breathes the Orlando Magic, and plays games with the minds of unsuspecting young women, including myself. Truth be told, I know better, but I have a few games of my own that I plan to play on him. Sean and I have been "friendly" off and on for about a year. I never expected much from the relationship, other than a "hook-up" here and there, but I at least thought he would respect me enough to call me back if I said it was important. Respect. Hmph. That's a strong word to use considering we never even defined our relationship or friendship until AFTER the deed was done. In case you didn't know, by then it's much too late. Whatever you don't talk about before sex, will never, ever, get talked about. Anyway, he hasn't been returning my calls for about a week. The sane part of me tells me to let it go and get myself another toy, but the other part of me says to call the man.

I scroll through my numbers and find his. Send. Rrring.

"Yeah?" By the sound of his voice, he had looked at his caller I.D. and didn't want to talk.

"Hey Sean," I said, trying to sound indifferent.

"Who is this?" he demanded, although I'm sure he already knew, he just wanted me to feel small. It worked.

"Gina," I said loudly.

"Oh, Whassup?"

"Nothing Sean, what happened to you the other night?" He was supposed to come over after the game and practice his, um, lay-ups. Guess I got traded.

"Oh, I must've fell asleep or something- who is this again?"

Dang. Did he have so many women that he couldn't keep it straight? I doubt if that's the case, he was just trying to make me feel small again. It worked again.

"This is Gina, Sean, look did I catch you at a bad time?"

"Yeah, kinda, I was on my way to Jay's Place."

Jay's place is a little club off of Arlington Expressway that has a sort of hip-hop/reggae/R&B vibe going on. It's a cool place, but did he really have to dis me to get there.

"I'll stop by when I get done Gina," he added, sucking his teeth like some leftover pork chop meat is in his teeth.

"Okay," I said too quickly. That actually appeased me. Damn, I know I couldn't be that desperate. I go to the bathroom to wash the Skin Success fade cream from my face and neck. I started using this stuff when I moved to Florida. They ain't never lied about Florida being the Sunshine State. Anyway, I don't want Sean to taste it when he kisses all over me, which I know he will. I take off my black doo rag and pull my chin length hair back into a ponytail, then decide I still look to plain. I put on some MAC blot powder to give my dark skin that "finished" look and some cotton candy flavored lip-gloss. I pop in my contacts so I can see every inch of that fine, black man when he, as my mother puts it, darkens my door. I slide out of my pajamas and put on a slinky black number. Easy access. No sense making the man struggle for what he is going to get any way. I run around the apartment and do a little "top cleaning"-that is, I throw my cosmetics, shoes, books, hangers-whatever-into a clothes basket and throw it in my closet. Sean is a neat freak, so I always comply. I glance at the clock on my night stand, the red digits blare 11:36. He'll be here by 2:30. Just enough time to take a good nap. You know, get my energy up.

Truth Hurts

Serena had been my best friend since high school, so it was not out of the ordinary for me to call her long distance early in the morning just to spill the details of my rendezvous.

"Whassup Serena", I chirped.

"Girrrrl, how did I know this was you? What have you done now?" Serena always talked to me in a condescending way when she felt I was up to something.

"Whhaaat? I was just calling to say hi since I ain't heard from you in foreva."

"You screwed him again didn't you?"

"Yeah, Serena, but I didn't call you to talk about that." Actually I did. I always felt giddy after he left and had to call somebody.

"Girl, you will learn someday."
I hate when she does that. She tends to forget that I learned my ways from her in the first place. Now she wants to be all judgmental. Serena has done this to me ever since we were in high school back in Georgia. How we remain friends is a mystery to me. Nevertheless, that's my dawg.

"Serena, don't start that right now? Please. I'm handling this situation and you know I don't want nothing from him, so what do I have to lose?"

"Just remember G, you said the same thing about Lance."
Why did I even call her? Sometimes I think she savors the fact that somebody's life could be as messed up as hers.

"No," I corrected her, "Lance was MY man, so there is a whole lotta difference. You can't compare apples with oranges, damn."

Lance had been my off again-on again boyfriend for
four years in college. Lance was a dysfunctional
Architect/Artist/Entrepreneur/Unemployed broke
ass hustler that I loved from the crown of his head
to the soles of his feet. Lance and I had gone
through the valley together but never made it to the
mountain top. I found out that Lance had gotten
married two months prior to the last time I slept
with him. I was crushed. What kind of friend would
throw something like that in your face?

"Look Gina," she tried to calm me down, "I
just don't want you to get hurt, alright? Don't fool
yourself that you don't want this man."

"I want a lot of things, Serena. I want a
million dollars, but I know it's not my time to have
it yet. Same thing with Sean. I got everything on
lock. Hey, I'll call you later, somebody's at the
door."

"Well I hope it ain't him"

"Bye Serena."

"Bye Ho."

Nobody was at the door. Serena had sent me
into a mode of pissosity. Partly because she was
right and partly because it was none of her business.
I look at the apple shaped clock in my kitchen, it is
noon and I am damn glad I don't have to look at
that television station today. I love my job as
Production Supervisor, but Channel 4 can survive
without me today. I slide open my glass doors to let
some fresh air circulate through my apartment. I
then strip my hunter green sheets from my bed. I
notice a wet spot on the top sheet and sniff it.

"Sean is so stupid. I hate him," I say out
loud to nobody in particular. Then I pick up the
phone, hit *67 and call him to see if he answers.
Voice mail. He always puts the phone on voicemail

when he's with a woman. I wonder if he's somewhere making a woman climb the walls like he made me do last night. Why do I care anyway?

The ringing phone almost made me jump out of my skin. I have got to turn that thing down.

"Hello?"

"What'chu doing?" It was my sister Monica who lives about 30 minutes from me in St. Marys, Georgia. She's four years older than me, and so much more together than me. She's been married to her husband, Kamar, for about 5 years. They have two rug rats, Demetria and Eric, 5 and 3.

"Nothing, just cleaning up a little bit."

"Oh. Well me, Demetria and Eric getting ready to head out that way to go to the mall, wanna come?"

"Naw, y'all go ahead, my head look a mess and I need to finish cleaning and stuff."

"Alright, I'll holla back at'cha later."

"I'll be here," I said and rolled my eyes. Rolled my eyes because she's just so damn together. I love my sister to death, but today I can't take being around the happy family. Not when I'm 24 without a man or a prospect. Not today when I just slept with fine ass "dead end" brother. Not today when I know she will be trying to push one of her husband's single, as in not married but perhaps involved with some chick, friends on me. Not today. I hang up the phone and tap my fingers on it for a minute. What should I do today? I look at my fingernails and remember why I hate wearing nail polish. My "Oh So Diva" berry color by Eleese is already chipping.

"This looks gross." I say out loud as I stand up from the bed to get the nail polish remover from the cabinet under the bathroom sink. I feel a squish under my foot. I look down. It's the used condom Mr. Neat Freak had left on the floor. I pick it up and hold it up toward the light to examine it. It's empty. As always. Sean hates to wear condoms and always manages to take it off mid act. I never stop him, which makes me just as stupid as he is. Is it really worth dying for? I ask myself that every time but never change my ways. I find the gold Magnum wrapper and drop it in the trash with the condom. I smile and shiver as I reminisce about the love that was made here last night. I hear Sean's voice over and over in my head singing "lord ha' mercy Gina, lord ha' mercy." How ironic for him to be asking the lord to have mercy on him as he boned my back out. Did I say love?

I switch my stereo on and quickly off again when I hear "Walk it Out". I like a little hip-hop every now and then as much as the rest of them, but not thirty times a day. Damn. The Deejays here really need to get a clue. I pop in a Joshua Redman CD and pump up the volume. Jazz always gets me going. I sway to the rhythm as I straighten the puffy green and wine colored comforter on my bed, the wal-mart print that everybody and their mama has, and fluff my pillows. The phone again. Who now?

"Whaaaat?" I say out loud before picking up the phone. "Hello," I say as I plop across my freshly made bed.

"Come and give me some head". It was Sean.

"What?" I chirped trying unsuccessfully not to sound happy.

"Come and give me some before I go to Carolina." He said in the same monotone as before.

"When you leaving?" I said ignoring his demand.

"In a little bit. You gon' come hook a brother up or what?"

"Why you can't come by and hook ME up." I whined. I hate whining.

"I'ah be there in a minute."

Damn I'm good. Brother can't stay away for four hours before he need another taste of the goodies. I run to the bathroom and grab my washcloth to give down there some quick attention. If I'm gon' get hooked up, I'm gon' smell like Dove and Strawberries. I'm glad I beveled my hair this morning. I grab my blot powder and "Oh baby" lip gloss by MAC. It tastes like chocolate and Sean loves to suck on my lips when I wear it. I spray the air with some Glade Neutralizer because I hate those flowery fragrances. I turn the air up on full blast because I know it's about to get hot in here.

My heart speeds up when I hear the thump of his music from the truck. I try to wait five seconds after I hear his impatient knock to open the door. One-one thousand, two-one thousand, three-one thousand—forget it.

"Who's there?"

"Sean."

I swing the door open nonchalantly and close and lock it behind him.

"Whassup" he sang looking down at me with that lethal smile he has.

"Whassup," I shoot back at him with an equally devious grin. He grabs the back of my neck with his humongous hands and pulls me into him. He's already rock hard and poking me right below my breasts. Without words, he leads me to the couch, frees my left breast and kisses it so gently that I melt and sink down into the cushions. He slowly works his way up my neck and to my lips. I whimper so quietly that I doubt if he heard me. I find his penis with my right hand and work it through his black nylon Nike shorts. He frees it for me and I instinctively lean down and start tongue kissing his love wand. Shit Gina Shit Gina Shit Gina he sang while twitching his hands like he wanted to grab something. Anything.

"Arrggh." He roared like and attacking tiger and I'm his prey. He flips me over and rips my Bali panties from under my bright yellow sundress and kissing my diamond like there is no tomorrow. I'm floating. Spiraling. As soon as he feels my right leg shiver like it always does before I reach my moment, he comes up and plunges inside me. Fast and furious until we reach the top together. Not a break for a condom or a word. After our bodies stop shivering, Sean goes straight to the shower. After fifteen minutes of that awful singing he does, he comes out dressed. I pretend to be preoccupied with a rerun episode of "Martin" on Television. I don't know how that show lasted so long. He's so bafoonish. I can't lie though, I love me some Shenay-nay.

"I gotta go baby." He kisses me on my forehead. I saw *The Best Man*, I know about the forehead kiss.

"Alright." I fake indifference, but I'm really pissed. What the hell just happened here? I go to check the dresser for some money because this feels like a scene from Moulin Rouge. Damn.

Like Hell

The *Girlfriends* theme song blaring on my 27 inch cheap ass Magnavox lets me know that it is 5:30 already as I walk through the front door. Dang where has the day gone? The highlight of my day was finding boneless chicken breasts on sale at Winn   Dixie. They got damn near everything buy one get one free with those little cards. What's up with that? My paranoid brother in law says it's a conspiracy to find out what people buy to survive, then use it as leverage to kill us all. I think he spent too much time in the gulf war. I drop my bags on the counter to go pee.

"Whooo!" I sing out as I wipe too hard with the tissue. I forgot that my precious diamond is still tender from the two day Sean Olympics. I don't know why I continue to see Sean. I am tired of this same old tired scene. I need to get this off my chest. I pick up my cordless phone and hit Memory 1. Rring.

"Yeah?"

"Sean," I hesitated.

"Whassup baby?"

"Sean I'm tired of this shit."

"What 'chu talkin' bout?" He sounded like he was really confused.

"Sean, don't play me. I'm tired of sleeping with you and then feeling like this."

"Feeling like what Gina? Tell me whassup now because I'm tired and I don't need this right now. What'chu wanna do?"

"I want to stop this. I want some respect." There, I said it. "I want to have something to talk about other than sleeping together."

"Oh yeah?" He had the audacity to chuckle with it. "Well talk to me baby."

"Don't patronize me Sean, I'm serious.

"Look, Gina, we talk about stuff, you know this. I tell you shit that I don't tell nobody else. You can't respect that. What? You wanna go out or something?"

Now we are getting somewhere. Let me play this cool.

"Not like that Sean, just call me sometimes when your piece ain't hard. It don't have to be nothing special. I'm not trying to be your girlfriend or anything, but if you gon' be banging my back out on the regular, a cordial call sometimes would be nice."

"Oh, I be bangin' your back out?" He laughed trying to make me ease up. The lightness of his voice kinda made me laugh too.

"For real Sean, I want a little respect, you know?"

"I feel you. My bad. I'll make it up to you when I get back from South Carolina. I'm just really busy a lot I thought you knew that. It's not like that, alright?"

"Alright." I felt my tension calm down.

"You straight?" He sounded sincere.

"Yeah, talk to you later."

"Peace."

I feel better having spoken up. But you never know with Sean. He may have heard me, but odds are he didn't. Regardless, it's Friday and I want to have a good weekend so I decide to leave well enough alone.

"Shooooot, I want to kick it tonight." I say out loud as a flipped open the *Weekend Folio* paper that I picked up earlier. Absentmindedly turning the pages, I think about what I could possibly get into tonight. I look down at my bare feet. I should have gotten a pedicure while I was out today. I go to the bathroom, lean over the tub and run a warm, more like hot, bath. I grab my cell and quickly put it down realizing it's not 9pm yet. No calls during peak hours for me. I've got to get rid of T-mobile. I'm still recovering from a big ass bill last month. I grab my Vtech cordless phone with the scotch tape holding the batteries in it and call my girl Sharon.

"Wzup Share?" I quipped, "You sleep?"

"Hell yeah, I guess you can tell I don't have a life. It's Friday and I'm layed up on the sofa sleep like somebody's grandma," She laughed.

"Well I must not have one either 'cause I'm calling you. Girl let's go somewhere tonight," I say as I run a little water in my Origins ginger bubble bath to get the last little bit out.

"Where you wanna go? This is Jacksonville, ain't like we got a million choices."

"There you go, Sharon, I told you it's all about what you make it to be. Shoot, what about that little joint out in San Marco?"

"What you talking about Gina, *Olivia's*?

"Yeah, that's the one. I hear that's where all the chocolate eye candy be on a Friday night."

"Alright, you coming to get me?"

"Hell no Sharon, lets meet there, you know true playas ride solo." I was serious about that . An older brother once told me that he was much more likely to approach a sister who walked in the club alone rather than one that walked in with a whole entourage of chicks. I think I also read that in a book they call *The Rules* or something like that. But what do they know? If they had a man they would not have all that free time to be writing books.

"Bye Skank," Sharon said in her mad voice, "call me when you get ready to leave."

I light my jasmine scented candles and slide out of my jeans and orange Savannah State t-shirt and into my bathtub. The thing a love most about this apartment is the cobalt blue garden tub. This is my place of solace. The fact that I pay a grip for this one bedroom doesn't bother me as long as I have peace of mind, which this bathtub provides for me. I grab my foot file, pumice stone, and peppermint oil from the big basket beside the tub. No club is going to see my feet looking raggedy tonight. Bad enough Sean saw them. Like he cared anyway. I sink down into the steaming water and close my eyes. Like the old folks say, just resting my eyes. I must've drifted off to sleep because the ringing phone awakened me. Who is this calling me? Dang. I jump out of the tub dripping wet searching for my cell phone. I see it vibrating across my night stand and glowing blue.

"Hello?"

"Wzup Thicky Lake." It was Kiah, my ex-boyfriend from way back in the day. I'm talking high school sweetheart.

"Hey Kiah. I'll call you back, I'm in the tub."

"Naw-Naw-Naw. Talk to me now while you still dripping wet."
Kiah and I always played like that. He is the coolest ex I got. Were still friends and kick it every blue moon.

"Bye big head." I say. He knows I'll call him back.

"Bye crazy ass girl."

"He must be bored." I say out loud as I plop back down in the water. I love talking to Kiah, especially when I'm feeling down, but sometimes I think he's secretly glad that every relationship that I have had since him has failed miserably. Especially Lance. Kiah hated the hell out of him some Lance. He was so overjoyed when Lance treated me like shit. "You don't need him-you don't need him". It was like a song Kiah used to sing in my ear every time I mentioned Lance. He was right though, I didn't need him.

I find myself trying to picture what I'm going to wear tonight while sloughing dead skin off my feet and into the tub, which I'm now sitting on the side of because I have issues with anything besides soap being in my bath water. If even one piece of hair floats to the top of the water, I have to get out until I can get it out. I've been like that since I was a little girl. My mama says I'm "nice nasty". Everybody else says I'm just crazy as hell. I lean off the side of the tub and squint down at my cell phone to see what time it is. 9:52. I dry off my feet. I don't have time to polish my toes pretty, so a clear coat will have to do.

"Pretty enough." I say as I finish the job. If I'm lucky, the brothers will be paying attention to more than my feet anyway. I decide to wear my black sea pants with the little shimmies dangling from the bottom with my sheer Issye Miyake blouse. The one I spent my rent on. Hood rich. Damn I look good if I must so say myself. I'm glad Donatello, my hair stylist, talked me into letting him cut me some layers. His name is really Donald, but once he opened his own shop in midtowne he became the fabulous Donatello. Some people say he's gay but I think he's just funny as hell. I grab my purse and keys and head for the door. I decide to wait until I'm about halfway to the club before I call Sharon to let her know I'm leaving. I don't want her to get there first and be waiting on me in the parking lot looking scary, so I'll just get there first and go on in.

I wish this traffic light would just turn green. I'm gon' run it if it doesn't change in one minute. Rrring. Dang. Sharon.

"I was just getting ready to call you, Sharon, I'm walking out of the door right now." I lied. I was already half way there.

"Well I already left, I figured you were running late."

"If you get there first, go on in, I'll find you."

"Nu-unh Gina, we going' up in that piece together."

She is defeating the hell out of my purpose.

"Sharon, if I get there first, I'm going in. It's too dangerous to be standing around outside."

"Why you always do that Gina? You think the men all pause when you walk into the room, don't you?

"And you know this--- Man." I say imitating Chris Tucker with his fine self. "See you in a minute."

"Wait!" She scared me. "What's the cover charge tonight?"

I roll my eyes. For someone who always wants men to buy her Prada this and Gucci that, she is a cheap heifer when it comes to paying for things for herself.

"I'oun know Share, probably under 20 dollars."

"It better be, I ain't got BUT 20. Where your boy Sean at? Can't he get us on the VIP list?"

"Come on Sharon, don't start that. What-you mean Mr. Michael didn't break you off no coins this week?"

Michael is Sharon's-well, I don't know exactly what he is, but he is at her house everyday, all day, except Saturdays and Sundays. Where he goes on those days, I don't know. Whenever I ask Sharon, her response is, "don't know, don't care". Michael doesn't work, but Sharon say's that he's "from money", and is waiting on some big inheritance. Whatever. She's so gullible.

"Nope, his daughter is getting braces, so you know how that goes."
Did I mention that he is also somebody's daddy.

"Well Sharon you just gon' have to stop being cheap and come off that money tonight. You know you got it, you ain't letting' Blue Cross-Blue Shield pimp you for free are you. You been working mad overtime lately. And I sure as hell ain't paying for you." I was for real too.

"Alright hoochie, I hope you choke on your drink." She laughed, but I know the heifer meant it.

"And I hope you trip off them Payless shoes I know you got on," I shot back at her.

"Ha! They're Nine West. Bye!" She hung up before I could get the last word.

Pulling up to *Olivia's*, I regret that I didn't put my purse in the trunk before I got here. No use doing it now, it kind of defeats the purpose if everybody sees you do it. I tuck my purse under the seat. I decide to forgo the valet parking because Sheena, my black Mustang, is too dirty to be rolling' all up front and center. I take a look around at all the shades of chocolate, almond, toffee cream-you name it. These black people were dressed to the nines too. Not a hair out of place on anybody. This is the kind of crowd I like. I step out of the car and take one last glance at myself in the car window. I turn around and head toward the long ass line at the door. I wish Sean was here because I wouldn't have to wait in line. There is something kind of humbling-borderline humiliating about standing alone in a line waiting to go into a den of sin. At least the line seems to be moving pretty fast, I am already close enough to the door to feel the rush of heat from the inside. Is that somebody calling my name? I look back.

"Gina, wzup girl?"

I see a tall, nicely built piece of chocolate walking toward me. It's Darius, one of Sean's teammates. I wonder why they always come to Jacksonville to party and hang out. Maybe they've played themselves out in Orlando. I quickly look past him, secretly hoping to see Sean following him. No such luck.

"Hey Darius," I smile at him, embarrassed that I'm standing in the stupid line looking alone and lost.

"Come in with me, you ain't gotta wait in this line," he says.

"I don't mind waiting, I'm kind of enjoying the night air." I'm lying. Truth is, my feet are already hurting and the brothers behind me are smoking like a train and making comments about my booty. On top of that, this Florida humidity is making my hair stick to my face like I got some played out fingerwaves.

"Well come anyway," he says and grabs my hand pulling me to the front of the line. If looks could kill, I would be a dead mamma jamma the way these heifers are giving me the ice grill. Darius is a very well known point guard for the Magic, so I guess I was assumed to be one of the conquered.

"Waaaaiiit for me Gina!" Why lord, why? Who else? Sharon-running and tripping over her sandals looking like somebody is chasing her. I couldn't help but to laugh with everyone else in the line.

"Darius, that's my friend, can she come in with us?" I ask.

"Mo' ladies make it Mo' betta." He is so tired. Must be the NBA anthem.
When we finally get inside the club, Sharon's aggravating ass is pinching me on the back of my arm and whispering for me to introduce her to Darius. Really I was trying to avoid having to do that, but I go ahead and give in.

"Darius, this is my friend Sharon. Sharon-Darius." I say not really looking at either of them.

"*Very* pleased to meet you," Sharon says looking like a skinny ass hungry hippo. That was mean, but she doesn't have to make it so obvious that she is sweating him. I roll my eyes at her when he's not looking. She shoots me a quick bird.

"Likewise," Darius says as we try to avoid getting moved by the crowd of people trying to get past the little entry area we are standing in. When we finally turn the corner and approach the dance area, the heat slaps us harder than I've ever been slapped in real life.

"Dang, it's thick off in this piece," I whisper to Sharon as we both watch Darius stop and give dap to every other brother he walks by. "Let's go this way," I tell Sharon, motioning the opposite way from Darius.

"I thought we was with him," Sharon says looking like she still wants to follow him. My pride wouldn't let me. I didn't want to look like the groupie.

"I'm going to the bar, Share. You go ahead." I say as I turn and make my way through the crowd to the circular, brown leather trimmed bar. When I finally get to the bar, I turn and see Sharon right behind me, sweating and panting like a hot lion. That girl know she makes me laugh.

"I thought you was gon' hang with Mr. Darius," I say.

"Nah, that's *your* friend, I just wanted to drink for free," she says matter-of-factly.

"Girl, you are off the heezy," I yell to her over the music.
The bartender sits two red drinks in front of us.

"These aren't ours," I say.

"Free Alize' for the ladies until 12:30." He says. He kind of looks like that man that plays the daddy on that show where the little girl lives with her dad. I think it's called *One on One*.

"Thank ya!" Sharon yells like she just hit the lotto.

"Here, Share, you can have mine too. Alize makes me crazy." I spin around to the bartender. "Can I get a rum and coke?"

"Oh, Alize makes you crazy, but you can handle rum and coke?" Sharon quips. I had to laugh at that one myself. I really don't care for Alize' though, it tastes like poison to me-whatever poison tastes like in my mind. But I'm barely going to sip on this drink anyway, I'm trying to stay on my low-carb diet. The bartender sits the drink down in front of me and has the balls to ask me if it's on Darius' tab.

"No," I say while handing him a five dollar bill and looking him up and down. Who does he think I am, I don't need a man to pay for my drinks.

"My bad," he says apologetically, "I saw you come in with him. But rum and coke is 8 bucks."

"Well in that case, yeah this is on his tab," I say snatching back my five dollar bill. That's what I get for trying to be Ms. Women's Lib. Sharon and I walk away from the bar cracking up. "Look, there is an empty table-let's get it."

"Nu-unh Gina, I'm going to the dance floor." She insists.

"Ok, I'll just observe for a minute. Leave your drinks, I'll watch them." I really wanted her to put them down because she looked super ghetto drinking out of two glasses.

"Okay, but don't be sipping out my stuff," she says before disappearing into the crowd and laughing.

I sit down at the table and immediately realized that I should have gone with Sharon. I look like a drink-sitter sitting at this damn table with three drinks and two empty chairs. I quickly adjust my body language to look approachable. I remember reading that you should never fold your arms and should try to do something sensual with your hands. Sensual? Whatever. I grab my drink and sip as "sensually" as possible. Before I put it down, a short brother with some Iverson cornrows is standing in front of me. Dang, those anorexic heffas from Cosmo magazine might be onto something. No wonder they are pulling all the brothers. That thought makes me laugh a little.

"Well hello there," he grins. "Am I that funny looking?"

"Oh, no, sorry. I was just thinking about something," I manage, still smiling.

"Well can I sit down so you can share it with me?"

I gesture for him to sit down.

"Marcus Elliot," he introduces himself.

"Gina Anniston," I say and quickly regret having given him my real name.

"Gina. A beautiful name for a beautiful woman."

The look on my face must've told him that I was not impressed with that lame, old school line.

"I'm sorry," he laughed. "I couldn't resist."

"Yeah, I bet," I say still not impressed.

"Uh-oh," he says pointing to the drinks on the table. "Your man ain't gon' get mad about me sitting here talking to you over his drinks, is he?"

"If I was here with someone, trust me, I would have told you right away."

"Oh, well you know how *y'all* do it sometimes," he says.

Y'all? I'm not even going there with the brother. Y'all as in who? Women? Black women? I refuse to go there. I bob my head to the beat of Beyonce's *Get Me Bodied.* . One thing is for sure, this dude will not be getting me bodied tonight. I pretend to be interested in something across the room. Sensing that I'm not interested in him, he reaches into his pocket, pulls out a business card and places it in front of me.

"You can call me if you want to."

I nod silently with a half smile and look away again. As soon as he walks away, I drop his card in the ashtray, take a sip of my rum and coke, and head for the ladies room. Dang, this rum and coke got me kind of dizzy. By the time I get to the door of the ladies room, my vision is so blurry all I can do is lean against the wall and hold on. I look toward the dance floor to see if I can find Sharon. My chest feels tight. I try to remember the symptoms for a stroke or heart attack from my CPR class, but I'm drawing a blank. Just as I feel myself about to pass out, I feel somebody grab me around the waist and hold me up.

"You alright?" I hear a voice. It's ole boy with the cornrows from the table.

"I don't know," I manage. "Could you get my friend for me? She's right over there." I try to point toward the dance floor, but my arm feels heavy and weird.

"Maybe you just need some fresh air. Let me help you to the front door."
He pulls me in the opposite direction for Sharon, toward the front door. This doesn't feel right. Something's wrong. I can't keep my eyes open. The last thing I see is a flash and then I remember giving up and falling down. Blackness.

And Leads to Deception

I open my eyes and they are blurry. I squint and look around. I see a group of elephants charging at me. I jump and shriek. But wait, on second glance, they are miniature. I squint some more. It looks like they've stopped charging at me. Clarity sets in. They look like they might be a collection of elephant figurines, which must mean I'm at home. In my bedroom. I sit up and grab at my chest to see if I'm dressed. I have on my black PJ's.

"Hey sleepy head." That was Sharon. "Girl that rum and coke had you messed up like a mug at 'livia's. "You feel alright?" She didn't give me time to answer. "Your head gon' be hurting like a mofo in the morning."

Still dazed and confused a little bit, I ask, "What time is it?"
I hear a deep voice that startles the hell out of me.

"Lil' bit after 4 in the morning." That was Darius. What the hell was he doing in my apartment? I didn't even know he knew where I lived.

Sharon walks over to the side of my bed and plops down. "Girrrrrrl, you made a spectacle of yourself at that club tonight. I ain't never seen you drink enough to pass out. I didn't know you had it in you, Gina."

"What?" I manage to stammer. "I didn't drink but bout 3 sips of that rum and coke." I tried to sit up but my neck was stiff and sore. I must've fallen pretty hard. "How did I get home?"

"Oh. This fine, young, almondy brother with some cornrows was trying to help you when Darius saw you. Almondy was our way of saying pecan tan. He was trying to get you in his car so you could lie down in a safe place. Darius came and got me and we brought yo' drunk ass home."

It dawned on me immediately. That little punk had slipped me a mickey. I became frantic. I know that little bastard didn't touch me. Did he touch me? I screamed at Sharon and Darius.

"Where did y'all find me? Call the police! I need to go to the bathroom."

"Wait Gina! Chill. What's wrong?" Sharon was looking freaked out.

"That dude. He might have.. Oh my god. Did he slip something in my drink?"
Silence. We all just sit for a minute. Everyone was afraid to be the next to say something. Darius finally broke the spell.

"Gina you might need to go to the E.R. You think?" He is looking pretty freaked out too.

I sit up and look around for my purse. I remember where I left it.

"Where is my car y'all, my purse is in it?"

"We left it at the club G," Share said. "We rode in Darius' truck."

"I'll drive. We need to hurry up." Darius says while patting the pockets of his camel colored linen dress pants for his keys.

I get up slowly and head for the bathroom. I stop when I remember that you shouldn't go to the restroom when there's a possibility that you have been... I'm not even going to think like that. That bastard better not have touched me.

On the way to the hospital, I closed my eyes and tried to stay calm. This could be anything. Maybe I have some kind of illness that I'm unaware of. I don't remember exactly what happened at the club, and I'm afraid to ask. I hope I didn't lose it and make a big scene. Darius turns the music down and keeps glancing at me out of the corner of his eyes.

"What's wrong?" I ask feeling self conscious.

"Nuttin'. Just checking to see if you're alright." He said putting his eyes back on the road.

He probably was looking at me like that because Sean has told him how he turns me upside down, inside out, and 'round and 'round like Diana Ross. I wonder if men talk like that. I slide further down in the peanut butter leather seats and try not to feel so exposed. I grab my neck and rub it. Darius reaches over like he is going to touch my neck. I jump.

"My bad, Gina, I was just going to adjust the neck rest for you." He gave me a strange look.

"Nah, it's cool. Just edgy I guess." I say feeling embarrassed.

I look in the rearview mirror and see Sharon with her head back. She appears to be sleeping. That's my girl. I know she's tired, but she wouldn't leave my side for all the tea in China right about now. Darius takes a quick glance at Sharon and see she's sleeping too.

"So what's up with you and my boy?" Darius asks trying to be nosy.

"Who Sean?" Like I don't know who he's talking about. "Me and Sean are cool. We just kick it sometimes. Why?"

He gives me one of those little chuckles that says he knows what I moan and chant, what kind of moves I make when my head is full of those pretty colors. Men.

"Just asking."

"Oh." I decide not to push this conversation any further.

It seems like it takes forever for them to call my name when we are sitting in the emergency room. I have to pee really bad and I'm tired and sleepy, and anxious all at the same time. On the little sign-in paper at the desk where it asks for symptoms, I wrote "passed out". Shouldn't they rush me back? Maybe I should have written "dead". The little lady with the dark pink pants, and colorful uniform top finally appears at the double doors and unemotionally calls my name. They put me in a room in the back that wasn't a room at all. It was a small section of a big, open area that was "closed" off by a curtain. I could hear everybody's diagnosis and business. The lady in the "curtain room" beside me had been admitted because her blood pressure shot way up after she ate some ribs at a bar-b-que. They had given her a diuretic and now she kept telling her husband she had to pee every 10 minutes. He was getting frustrated with her.

After the nurses had run a blood, urine, and every other kind of test they could think of on me, a young, black, male doctor appeared behind the curtain. I was happy that he was a brother. Sometimes you only feel like dealing with your own people. He had thick, curly, black hair. He was handsome. No ring. I couldn't help but to check for that.

"Ms. Anniston, how are you? I'm Dr. Long."
I bet you are.
"Hello, Doctor."
"Well I'll get straight to the point. We found traces of GHB in your urine. It appears to be a relatively small amount, so I don't think you'll have any further effects from it."
"What is GHB?" I cut him off.

"Well that's what I'm getting to. It is unfortunately commonly used as a sedative on rape victims."

I jumped and sat up straight. I grabbed my chest.

"Calm down Ms. Anniston, I don't think you were raped, but we would like to do another pelvic exam on you just as a precautionary measure."
Great. I went to the club in hopes of maybe meeting someone who could eventually be a booty friend. But this is not what I had in mind.

After my exam revealed that there were no traces of anybody's semen, thank God, or any traces of latex residue. I was free to go after having to explain to the doctor that the slight bruising on the walls of my vagina was due to my consensual sexcapade with Sean. On the way, the nurse introduced me to a police officer and explained that he would take my report for further investigation.

The officer was a nicely built black man, probably mid forties, with a sharp cut goatee, and of course that hideous blue uniform. Again, I was glad he was a brother. He seemed very concerned as I gave him the story, and a description of the person I suspect did this crap. After I told him the whole story about brother-man with the Iverson braids, he wrote up his little report on his clip board and thanked me for me time. He said the detectives would be in touch with me later in case I remembered anything else.

That's it? No entourage of police officers in heavy gear scouring the streets to find this punk and lock him under the jail? No SWAT team? They don't care. This is another one for the file. I straighten up my jeans and wrinkled t-shirt, which I picked up from the floor and threw on in the rush to get here, and push the buzzer for the receptionist to buzz me the hell up out of here. I feel raped. Not sexually. Just raped by the fact that someone that I don't know did something to me that I have absolutely no control over. Women catch hell 24/7/365. And nobody seems to care one way or the other.

Opportunity's Impatient Knock

A ringing phone jars me from my sleep. I peer at the red glowing digits. 8:45 Am. I've only been asleep for an hour, but it feels like longer. It's Sean.

"Hey baby, you alright? Darius called me at like 6 this morning and said you were at the hospital."

I knew he cared.

"Yeah, I'm cool. Just a little banged up." I try to sound more pitiful than I actually am. Might as well milk it for all it's worth. "Are you still in South Carolina?"

"Nah, I'm on my way back. I just had to check on my peeps real quick."

I figured that meant he had to check on some chick from back home who was sitting up under his family, waiting to become an NBA wife. Heifer.

"Oh." I say, weakly. I'm so devious.

"You need anything?" He sounds sincere. But then again, this *is* Sean.

"No, I'm just gon' stay in the bed all day and rest." I tried to emphasize the word bed so he would get a subliminal message.

"You want me to come by?"

"Yes." Damn. I answered too fast.

"Sit tight. I'm on the way."

Yes yes yes yes yes. I knew I went to that club for a reason. I'm tripping. I all of a sudden have the energy to get up and take a shower. It's amazing what the thought of a 6'5 chocolate bar will make you do.

I decide to use regular Whitewater Zest. I didn't want to smell too extravagant so Sean would think I was doing it all for him. Getting out of the shower, I really don't feel like putting on lotion, but I do anyway because skin contact is everything. I use Almond Cookie Butter by Carol's Daughter, my secret fragrance.

While pulling on my satin leopard print PJ's , I start to picture that short, cornrow wearing hustler that slipped me that mickey. Dang. He was a decent looking brother when I really thought about it. I'm sure there were several sisters in the club that would've gone home with him. Hell, approached right, I may have even given him my number. Thinking of him makes me want to get back in bed and pull the covers up over my head, so that's what I do.

I must've fallen hard asleep. Again the loud ringing phone makes me jump sky high.

"Hello?"

"It's me Gina. Open the gate." Sean. I press 9 on my phone and hang up when I heard the long beep signaling the gate opening.

I start to go to the mirror to check myself out, but decide to forgo it because I feel like crap anyway. I unlock the door before he even parks his SUV and then I crawl back into bed. I yell for him to come in when I hear that familiar impatient knock.

"Gina don't leave the damn door unlocked like that. Niggas will walk up in here on you quick."

In my head, he's fussing at me because he cares.

"I just unlocked it. I ain't crazy. Especially after last night."

"How do you feel?" He eases down on my bed. The same bed he's usually a wild man in.

"I'm cool. A little queasy in the stomach. Tired. But that's it."

"You eat yet?" He fumbles with my white porcelain elephant on my nightstand.

"Nah, not hungry. Leave my elephant alone. That is Lalique." I joke with him.

"That is La-cheap." He shoots back and we both crack up. He is so lame.

He takes off his black G-Unit sneakers and puts them neatly beside my bed. He shimmies out of his gray sweats and folds them neatly, laying them on the dresser. Takes the cover back on the other side of the bed and eases in. I instinctively turn over and he spoons me from behind. No words. We silently watch a lady wearing purple stretch pants and a lavender sweatshirt with purple flowers win a purple Dodge Neon on *The Price is Right*.

I realize something while laying in Sean's arms. My best friend Serena was right. It **is** more than the sex. I like Sean. A lot. Enough to do battle with ole girl from back home. The "peeps" that he had to check on. She may be a figment of my creativity, or she may be real. Either way, that heifer is in for a battle. And I don't plan on losing.

. "I'm hungry Sean." I say as the Barker Babes wave goodbye.

"I gotta sausage for you."

He is so stupid.

"For real Sean."

"Me too. Get up and cook." He says while pushing me out of bed.

"I'm sick Sean, you cook." I whine. I really hate whiners. I don't know why I do it.

"Ain't nuttin' wrong with you but evil as hell girl."

I push him off the side of the bed and go to the bathroom to pee. When I come back, he's laying in the middle of my bed-butt naked and stroking his rock hard piece.

"Sean, stop that." I say frowning.

"Come help me Gina. Look how hard it is baby." Now he was whining and swinging it back and forth. I look at him, laugh and then head for the kitchen to look for something to eat. I know he's going to follow me. As soon as I open the fridge and bend down to look in the veggie bin, I feel it poking me from behind. I laugh and turn around and push him away.

"Later, Sean. I gotta eat. I'm feeling funny."

"Gina, you know what you do to me, c'mon now."

"Yeah me and everybody else." I try to mumble but apparently he can hear very well.

"Why ya'll always gotta say stuff like that?" He spoke too quickly and realized it a second too late. I caught it immediately. He said *y'all*. That meant that every woman he was dealing with was concerned about what he was doing with other women. Once again, I start to wonder why I even deal with him anyway. I totally realize that I am setting myself up for heartbreak. Yet I continue to fool myself that I just want to be his friend.

I choose not to even respond to Sean's comment. I find the grits and take out my chrome quart sized pot and partially fill it with water.

"Sean, you want grits?" I ask dryly.

"Grits? Is that all you gon' cook? You call yourself a Georgia peach right?"
His lighthearted conversation makes me forget a little and ease up.

"I'mma cook some eggs, turkey bacon, and French toast too," I say while pulling up my PJ top and scratching my side. I must've missed a spot with the lotion.

"Yeah, that's what I'm talking 'bout. Mama always told me to find a thick ass Georgia girl if I wanna eat well," he says through that crooked, sexy, smile of his.

"You know it," I say proudly. I'm not one of those new millennium chicks who thinks I'm too cute to boil water. I can turn a kitchen out.

Sean finds a spot on the floor in front of TV. He finds my universal remote and clicks until he stops on *The View*. I can't believe he's interested. I'm impressed.

"Sean, I didn't know you watched talk shows."

"Nah," he leaned back on my camel colored sofa cushion. "It's like a peep show because that new thick girl's legs never quite close all the way underneath that table. Plus Whoopie is looking kinda fly in her old age."
He's so damn silly.

"Whatever," I say, rolling my eyes at him. "Food's ready."

"Fix me a plate," he says without looking back.

"Don't get ridiculous," I say, fixing the plate for him anyway. I imagine what it would be like to be married to Sean and cook for him everyday, but quickly shoot the thought from my head and hand him the extra large plate and a fork. Since he was going to eat in front of the TV. I decided to get my plate and join him.

After having our breakfast/lunch/brunch and watching a couple of old North Carolina State basketball games on ESPN Classic, Sean stands up, stretches and says he needs to go get his workout on. I crotch watch for a second and regret not letting him get his workout on earlier. That man know he has some stamina. Feeling a little better myself, I decide to go into the station-something I rarely do on a Saturday, and catch up on some work.

Pulling into the station, I think to myself that I should've called to let them know I was coming so the production crew wouldn't think I was trying to sneak in and check up on them.

"Oh well, they'll just have to get over it," I say to myself aloud as I dig through my junky purse to find my electronic access key. I really need to organize more.

Walking through the huge glass doors in the front of the 7 story, red brick front building, I see my coworker, Shoney. Shoney is a sister, and the best camera person in the building. Black, white, man, woman-doesn't matter- Shoney's the best. She's walking with one of my not-so-favorite people, Marilyn, an administrative assistant. Marilyn thinks that sun rises and sets on her white ass.

"Afternoon ladies." I say as I stop in front of the lobby's cork bulletin board to remove old memos- a job the PA's –production assistants- are supposed to handle.

"Hey girl. You back from your hiatus?" Shoney joked. I had only been gone two days.

"Hmph," Marilyn murmurs, looking around for something to scrutinize. I looked directly at Shoney, hoping Marilyn would disappear from my peripheral view.

"Girrrrl, we'll talk later. Drama." I whisper to her like she and I are the only ones standing there.

Marilyn cut in with, "Seems like people around here *thrive* on drama."
Shoney and exchange looks.

"Nice shoes," I tell Marilyn, changing the subject. They really were nice leather pumps. Too bad she's wearing them with that tacky green suit from One Price Fashions. I don't care what anybody says, expensive shoes will not make a tore up outfit look good.

"Well ladies," I say making my departure, "I would love to stay and chat but I need to catch up on some paperwork."

"Let's do lunch." Shoney calls behind me.

"Call me." I say, making the phone to ear motion without looking back. Shoney is tall, dark chocolate, and thin as a whistle. All the men at the station, most of whom are white, love them some Shoney. I like hanging out with Shoney because she carries such positive energy. She seems to attract positive people, too. Which is why I can't figure out why she chooses to associate herself with that trifling Marilyn.

Marilyn and I started out having a strictly business-"hi and bye"-relationship. Being that she was always with Shoney, I assumed she was cool so I started to lengthen our "hi's and bye's". Big mistake. Marilyn is one of the most toxic people I have ever come across. There is always something wrong with her. Always complaining. Forever saying people are jealous of her because she drives a Lexus. A 1993 Lexus. I kind of feel sorry for Marilyn because she seems so unhappy with herself. Maybe because she isn't in the place she thought she'd be at 50 years old. But hell, is anybody in the place they want to be? No, but that's a good thing because it creates drive and motivation. It would serve her better to do something about it other than complain, though. She even once had the audacity to tell me not to get too comfortable in my "little supervisor position", and that she'd seen more than her fair share of young supervisors come and go. She also advised me to chill on wearing so many designer suits and purses because quote, "You're not impressing anybody; you are turning them against you."

That conversation stayed in my head a long time, but little did Marilyn know that my suits were not expensive designer suits. My shit comes from JC Penney and Steve and Barry's like a mug. And as far as handbags, the little Korean lady down at Fashion Town knows me well. My purses come from right beside the Motions Permanent Relaxer section. I couldn't believe Marilyn had sweated me like that. It hadn't helped that Shoney had mentioned Sean to her. I'm not even dating Sean, but Shoney had made it seem like he and I were on the verge of matrimony. Marilyn couldn't stand it. She had even gone on a mini rampage one day about her friend that works at the free clinic telling her how many pro ball-players in this city are HIV positive. She had "threatened" to name drop, but didn't want her friend to lose her job over spilling the beans. I had to laugh. Why would a pro-baller need to go to the free clinic?
She went on to say that she wouldn't let a pro athlete touch her with a 10 foot pole. I doubt she would ever have that problem.

It's about time for the 4 o'clock broadcast; I take a seat in one of the big, orange fluffy chairs in the lobby to watch, instead of going into the studio. I'm a full time procrastinator.

Sitting in the chair absently minded watching Chad Lumpkins, a news anchor, tell a story about public dumping, my mind drifted back to Sean. I need a new hobby. My phone breaks my thoughts by playing "Remember" by Keyshia Cole and vibrating on my lap. The caller I.D. says "bonehead". It's Sharon.

"Yeah," I answer.

"Girl where you at?" She's screaming into the phone. I cringe.

"Stop yelling. I'm at work. What's up?"

"At work? Are you crazy? You scared me half to death. I stopped by your apartment and freaked out when you weren't there. Thought you went back to the E.R."

"Nah, just came in to do a little work," I say, even though I'm chilling instead of working.

"How you feeling?" She asks, sounding like she's brushing her teeth.

"Oh. Better. Sean came by to check on me this morning," I gloat.

"No wonder you didn't call me. Heifer. You was getting *checked on*," she jokes.

"Ha. Ha," I laugh dryly. "I'll call you back. I'm knee deep in paperwork," I lie. But I really need to get moving today.

When I finally make it to my office, I close my door and put my phone on silent so as not to be bothered. By the time I look up again, it is 7:00pm. While gathering up some files to take home, I see the blue glow of my cell phone. The caller I.D says "Sean Home"'. Sean rarely calls me from home. The tiny print on the bottom left corner of my phone screen says 8 missed calls.

"Yeah," I say, fumbling to keep from dropping my folders.

"Gina did I leave my cell phone at your house?" He asks.

"I don't know, I'm at work."

"I've been calling you all day. I realized I didn't have it after I worked out. Came by the apartment too."

"I'll be leaving here in about an hour, Sean," I lied. "You can meet me at home at about 8:30 to see."

"Ahhh. A'ight. Peace."

I was lying my butt off. I would be home in about 15 minutes praying that the phone is there so I can go through his numbers and see what's really up. I may even have time to check a message or two.

Not Unanswered

I swerve into my apartment so fast that I almost run into the huge, black iron gate. I run up the three flights of stairs so fast that I miss a step and land on my knees. Without thinking twice or caring who the hell saw me, I hop right up and pounce like a cat to the top of the stairs.

"Hurry hurry hurry" I tell myself as I fumble with the door key, like someone is chasing me. Finally I swing the door open like that crazy ass white girl, Sidney, from *Scream*, the movie. As soon as the door bounces off that little door stopper thing behind it, I spot the phone. You know that music that plays on cartoons when the glow from heaven comes down? I swear I hear it while looking at that little silver Samsung laying on the floor.

I lock the door behind me and pick up the phone gently, as if I might hurt it if I handle it roughly. Jackpot. It had *4 messages* typed across the screen. Without hesitation, I dial *99 send, which is the code for most messaging systems. I grab a pen and paper from inside the "hideaway" part of my cherry coffee table to write down "important information". I impatiently listen to the little white lady say "You-have-4-new-messages. Press 3 to listen."

To my disappointment, the first message is from his loud mouth sister asking for 400 dollars for a doctor bill. Message two is her again saying she ran into one of his old classmates who wanted to know if he'd be able to get some free tickets. I pressed 5 to save her messages as new.

Message 3. Bullseye. "Sean, you didn't answer your phone last night so I guess you was with one of your hood rat hoes. Anyway this is

Trisha and you know why I'm calling. When you get a taste for some of this good stuff, holla. In case yo' trifling ass forgot the number, its-." I press 7 to erase. I didn't even bother to write her number down. I couldn't believe Sean had the low-life-ness to go there.

Message 4. "Hey babe." Excuse me? Did this heifer say 'babe'? "It's me. Just calling to see if you're feeling better." I wasn't aware anything was wrong with him.
"I miss you soooo much." Just as I thought, a chick from back home. "I can't wait to see you again. Thanks for the bracelet. Love you."

Stunned. Can't move. Love? I'm fuming mad. I know Sean is not my man but my feelings are still hurt like hell. How could he hold me like that and have someone else love him? And he bought her a bracelet. I bet it's laced with diamonds from all over the universe. Hell, I've been giving him the most precious diamond in the world anytime he wanted it, and what had he given me? His ass to kiss. Now I'm sitting here with a lump in my throat the size of Amelia Island. It's taking all I have not to cry, but I refuse. Why am I reacting like this? I should've known. I mean, I guess I did know, but it hurts like a mug now that I *know it* know it.

Okay G, just pull it together. Write the number down and figure out what to do later. I press the arrow button for missed calls. I see the number that corresponds with her call time and scribble it down. I double check to make sure I got it right. I put the phone back down on the floor in the exact spot I found it. I sit on the sofa and fix my eyes on the phone. It has betrayed me. I decide to wait a little while before calling Sean to let him know I found the phone. My mind starts to drift. I picture 'Ms. Thing' sitting at home in the middle of the day admiring her kazillion carat diamond bracelet. I picture Sean smiling and eating up my damn turkey bacon and grits this morning. Where was 'Ms. Thing' then? Just as I start trying to picture the other ghetto hooch that had left a message, my thoughts are interrupted by the white glow of Sean's phone. He had left it on silent. I pause for a split second and then jump up to look at the caller I.D. You would not believe the very number I had just written down was flashing across the screen. Sean is smart. No name is programmed with it.

My mind is running a million miles a minute. Gotta think quick. I can't answer it, Sean would never forgive me. Thinking like only a true sista' could, I hit the "talk" button and listened for a second.

"Sean? Sean?" I already hate her voice. I lay the phone down, still on, and start working on my stage skills.

"Stop Sean," I say in my cutest voice and try to make it sound like some tussling is going on. "Stop boy-you so crazy." I peep at the phone to see if she is still listening. Of course she is. I quiet down for 5 seconds, to make her imagination wander. Then I let her rip with fake sex moans.

"Ooooh. Ummmm. Mmmm. Sean baby. Mmmm." I slap my thigh hard and rhythmically to make 'Ms. Thing' think he was banging the hell out of me. I even go so far as to deepen my voice and grunt like Sean always did. More acting. "Sean-wait-I'm laying on the phone. Umph. Sean-wait baby." I slap my thigh even harder and faster to make it seem like he's too excited to stop. I pick up the phone to hear if she is saying anything. Boy is she ever.

"Sean," she's hysterical. "Sean! You bastard-stop it-how could you do this. I can't believe this-oh God oh God help me." She sounds so stupid screaming like he can really hear her. I press *end* with a smirk on my face. I start to feel bad for a second. That is, until the stupid heifer calls right back. Three times back to back to back. Okay now what do I do? As soon as Sean walks in the door, the phone will ring, she will spiel the story to him and he will know how stupid I really am. I need to fix this really fast. Now *my* phone is ringing. It's Sean.

"Hey Sean, I'm leaving the office now. Meet me in 15 minutes." I feel myself panicking.

"A'ight."

Shit shit shit. Two minutes pass. Then I'm thinking like a true playa again. There is no way Sean is going to answer his phone in my presence, especially if it's her, so I'm not in danger of him finding out right away. All I have to do now is make sure that everything that I pretended happened-happens. Okay here's the plan: As soon as Sean hits the door, I will start seducing him. I'll make sure we end up on the floor-on the cell phone, so I can say "wait, Sean, I'm on the phone," mid-act. Then when he gets up to go shower, which he always does, I'll get his phone and erase all the messages, which will probably number 100 by then. By the time she gets a chance to talk to him, everything she tells him will be the truth. Damn. If only I could use this power for good instead of evil.

Predator

My plan worked like a charm. Sean fell right into my trap and walked out of my door sexually satisfied and just as clueless as when he walked in. I feel like Stephan from "Days of Our Lives". I need to call somebody.

"Serena, wzup?" I say.

"Girl nothing. What's up with you? You didn't call me back the other day."

"Oh nothing. But Serena I did something really trifling." My voice trails off.

"Let me guess. It involves Sean." She does not sound enthused. Why did I even call her? For whatever reason, she is always on the defensive team when it comes to Sean. I think she is jealous of the possibility of me ending up with him.

"Nah, Serena," I lie, "nothing like that. I took an old dress back to Macy's and got my money back. I have worn that old thing a thousand times." I couldn't think of anything else trifling to say.

"Humph. You shouldn't have to do that if you messing with all the ballers you say you are." She laughs to try to make light of it but I know the heifer is serious. Since she wants to play, I'll join her.

"Oh girl, speaking of that, I meant to call you earlier to tell you about the diamond bracelet he bought for me." Well, he did buy a bracelet. Just not for me.

"For real? Umph. Must be nice."

"Girrrl, it is. The diamonds are huge. Certified clear." More lies.

"Dang, Gina. What made him buy that? Guilt?" I knew she would find a way to try to kill it for me.

"Nah, girl. The other day after I spoke to you, he and I were out shopping and when we got back in the car he whipped it out." What can I say? When you start lying it sort of snowballs.

Silence.

"Well Serena how's Lenny?" Her non working, woman chasing, low-life husband.

"Girl, he's fine. He's out looking for us a new living room suite."

I couldn't help but to laugh at my friend. She is still naïve as hell. It's Ten O'clock at night.

"Why didn't you go with him?" I try to wake her up.

"Oh, he wants to surprise me."

I gotta surprise for you, I think in my head, Lenny ain't at no damn furniture store.

"Well I'm sure he will pick out something cute." I wasn't talking about sofas.

"Yeah, he will." She's glowing over the phone.

"Okay girl. I just had to share that funny bit wit'cha. Talk with ya soon." Fake kisses. Our friendship is drifting.

Serena was not the person to tell what I had done to Sean. She's too judgmental these days. And starting to become unlikable. It's amazing how bitter a woman can become when she's with a no-good man. And who am I to talk?

I start to call Sharon but put the phone down mid-dial. I decide to keep this one on ice for a minute. I need to see how it's going to pan out anyway.

I tap my fingers on the coffee table. My gaze off into space is interrupted by a burning sensation on my right knee. I look down and see a small patch where the skin is a series of broken lines. Must've happened when I missed that step trying to beat Sean here. Looking at the exposed flesh made me remember that I had, once again, slept with Sean without a condom. Stupid stupid stupid. Not only am I well aware that 1 in 50 people in Florida are infected with HIV/AIDS, but I had also just found out that he is sexually involved with at least 2 other women. At least. One of whom I'm sure was your basic groupie/hood rat.

I get up and feel my bones pop. Sean's perspiration is still on me. I go into the bathroom and turn on the shower as hot as I can stand it. I scrub harder and harder trying to wash his everything off me. I try to wash 'Ms. Thing' and 'hood rat' off me. No amount of scrubbing is doing the trick. My skin feels raw. I jump out of the shower and look in the medicine cabinet for some Summer's Eve. I still feel nasty.

After my shower I lay across my bed, still soaking wet and cry out loud. I scream and curse. And finally pray.

Dear God,

I know you know what I want to say right now. I don't know how to say it, so thank you for hearing me. Amen.

Right now I feel so small. I feel as though I have no control over my life. I have compromised my health to feel loved and wanted by someone who is not even concerned with me. Everything is looking clearer all of a sudden. I couldn't care less what the hood rat caller looks like. I want my integrity back. The first thing I need to do is go to my doctor and get tested for…everything I guess. But what would the doctors and nurses think of me?

What if I... what if I have something? It's all too overwhelming to think about right now.

I pick up the phone and call Hunan Palace, the Chinese restaurant down the street. I order Moo Shu chicken and shrimp toast. While waiting on the delivery man, I decide to change my bed linen. I feel like burning them or throwing them away, but instead I walk through the kitchen to the closet which is called a laundry room and drop them in the washer. I turn the knob to *hot*, and dump 3 capfuls of Tide with Bleach in and slam the top down.

When my food arrives, I decide to eat on the balcony, even though it is almost midnight. I need fresh air. I light two citronella candles and eat in silence. I breathe deeply trying to renew myself. After dinner, I go to bed on a full stomach. I know that is unhealthy but I figure the sooner I could get to sleep, the sooner this day would be over.

In my sleep, I dream that I live in an African Village and am about to be crowned a princess. Six gorgeous blue-black men are beating out a ceremonial rhythm on the drums. Suddenly, I realize that the ceremonial drums are coming from my living room. Someone is beating on my door. Frantically. I glance at the clock. Three forty-three A.M. A door knock at 3:43 means trouble. I pray that nobody is dead.

I muster up enough strength to roll out of bed and creep toward the front door. I pause when I reach the door and take a deep breath. As I stand on my tiptoes to look through the peep hole, I prepare myself to see a police officer standing there holding his blue hat to his chest, just as I had seen 5 years ago when my brother had been killed by a drunk driver. I peer through the hole while holding my hand to my chest. Instead of a police officer, I see Sean. Standing there looking paranoid and scared. One half of me says not to even open the door and deal with whatever drama he's bringing. The other half of me says to myself 'you started it'. Against my better judgment, I swing the door open. I don't even bother to greet him or ask what's wrong. I just step aside so he can come in.

"Gina. I, uh, I got a little problem."

"Sean, it's damn near 4 in the morning. It better be a big problem."

"Let's sit down, G." He is sweating bullets.

"I don't want to sit… look. What do you want? And how did you get in the gate?" I'm impatient.

His eyes fill with water and he starts to twitch around in attempt to stop the flow. Alright, here it comes.

"I-I been meaning to mention…well, not really but.. anyway this girl from back home, right?"

I don't offer a response. I stand still and hold a solemn face. He continues.

"She, see, she thinks were still together. Me and her, and uh, she tripping."

I was still silent.

"She, um, called earlier today and I think she heard what happened between me and you. You know, when we uh, you know."
I finally decided to speak up

"Is that all Sean?"

"Well, she made me give you her number to prove that, uh…"

"And you gave it her?" I ask.

"But G, see, you don't.. you don't unders.."
I cut him off.

"Get out, Sean."

"But Gina baby, it ain't about nothing like that. You know me and you have an understanding," he pleads.

"Get-out-of-my-house-Sean," I repeat without raising my voice.

"But G, what you gon' tell her when she calls?" He's damn near crying.

"The truth. That you are what you are and that she should get herself a check-up," I say, still not moving an inch or showing any emotion.
He turns toward the door, after looking at me for a moment in disbelief. He opens the door and pauses.

"I should have known. You just like them other bitches," he says while descending the stairs.

"And just like your mama. You got it from somewhere." And with that I close the door and that chapter of my life.

Prey

Sure enough, 'Ms. Thing' called my house bright and early the next morning. I told her she had the wrong number. I couldn't even be mad at the situation because I started the whole mess. Well, actually, Sean started it but had a starring role in it.

I flip on the T.V. to kill the quietness and waste some time while my oatmeal finishes cooking. I see Aaliyah's face across the screen. I can't believe it's already the 4 year anniversary of her death. She was such a beautiful and talented entertainer. This just reminds me that life is too short to waste another minute on Sean. My deep train of thought is broken by a stench. Damn. I burned my breakfast. I run to the kitchen-well actually take two giant leaps from the sofa to the stove –I really need a bigger apartment- and grab the scorching pot by the rubber handle and drop it into the sink. My eyes find the apple red clock-no time to correct this mess, it's already 6:45am. I run some water in the gunk, burnt mess and grab a pop-tart from the pantry. What a way to start the week. Then to top the morning off, I snag my Brown Sugar pantyhose on the stair railings. They're cheap, but they look so good on my thick legs. I just wish they didn't make that swish swish sound when I walk.

Traffic is a bear on the Arlington Expressway into town. I flip a couple of people off and lay on my horn when a Lil Kim wannabe be cuts me off in her Lexus truck that I know she paid for with the money she made from being a stripper. I zip back around her and flip her off too at the foot of the Matthews bridge. Why am I in such a foul mood this morning? I need to get to Starbucks and get me an Espresso and chill what they call the fuck out. I know I'm going to be late for work, but never the less I decide to go to Starbucks around the corner from my job and get in the 20 minute line.

After I park Sheena, my ride, in my parking space at work, I head around the corner to get my dose of the black stuff. While rumbling through my purse trying to scrap up my 5 bucks, I hear someone calling me.

"Hi-eee Gina!" It was Marilyn, the company asshole.

"Hi Marilyn," I say, trying to force a smile. She flips or stringy blond hair and continues the unwelcome conversation.

"I see you need coffee too," she fake laughs holding up her cup to show me hers.

GOD PLEASE LET THE TOP FALL OFF WHILE THAT CUP IS TILTED TOWARD HER.

I'm wrong for that.

GOD PLEASE FORGIVE ME FOR THAT EVIL PRAYER. AMEN.

"Yeah Marilyn, I do have to have my caffeine," I say.

"Okay hon. Well I'll let Bob know where you are."

She is such an asshole. Of course Bob is the boss and will be less than pleased to hear that not only am I late, but I am taking the luxury of getting some coffee on company time. Marilyn doesn't realize that Bob does not like her being his informant all the time about every little thing. He's very team-oriented and knows that she is a morale killer like a mug. I look at her in disgust as she bounces her skinny, pale ass off to go tell 'massa' where the slave girl is. I will not let her win this time. As soon as she turns the corner in her suit that cost only a couple of bucks more than her coffee, I dash around the building the other way and go in the back door to beat the heifer inside. Due to being very friendly and conversational with the custodial staff, I know about the freight elevators that they use to bring heavy equipment to the top floors. I hop on and press 3-my floor. This elevator is so slow and rickety. Lord just let me make it. I impatiently press 3 again. The doors finally open and I run through the dark, musty, freight hallway toward the door leading to the employee lounge area-a shortcut to my office. I knock over a waste basket on the way and make a mental note to clean it up later. I slow down to a walk as I approach Bob's office. His door is open. I reach in the trash can outside his door and grab some old paperwork and an empty Starbucks cup. Props. I drop my purse in.

"Morning Bob!" I say cheerily, interrupting him from his morning internet porn. He minimizes the screen-as always- and shoots back a nervous "Good Morning. What's up?"

"Nothing Bob, just taking a morning coffee break. I got here really early to catch up on some work."

"Ata girl Gina. I noticed your car here early. I wish more of my employees had your drive." His lying ass was double checking his computer screen to make sure I didn't catch his peep show. He probably just got here himself.

"Thanks, Bob. Oh, by the way, I saw Marilyn in the long line at Starbucks while I was on my break. She will probably be a little late."

"Oh really?" Bob says, lifting an eyebrow.

Just as I finished spitting out that lie, Marilyn walked-more like tripped around the corner and looked like a deer in headlights.

"Hey Marilyn. How's that coffee?" I taunted as I bounced away from Bob's door toward my office, fake coffee and work props in tow. Gina-1. Company asshole-0. I just hope nobody empties that trash before I go back to get my purse out.

When I finally get to my office, I plop down in my brown, soft leather chair and look at my "In" box. Full. Good, the day will go by faster. I check our morning numbers to be sure we are still ahead of channel 12. We are. I want to be on top of things for our 11:00 a.m. meeting. I slack some days, but I'll be damned if 'big brother' is going to know it. I get a call as soon as I get started working.

"Gina Anniston. May I help you?"

"Hey G, it's me, Sharon. What'chu doing?"

"Working." I say with an impatient twang in my voice.

"I was just gon' ask you if you want to catch a movie after work. I need to let loose." She sounded stressed.

"Cool, just call me lata' gata." I hang up before she answers. I'm trying to learn to not let other people monopolize my time during the work day.

The day really flew by. Aside from me almost getting caught by Bob getting my purse from the trash can, the day was pretty much uneventful. I did catch the company asshole watching me from a distance a couple of times though. She was probably thinking of a way to even up the score. She better ask somebody.

The drive home started out peaceful. More peaceful than usual. I was in chill mode as I listened to Aaliyah sing "One in a Million." Every station was giving mad props to her today. She deserves it.

I heard her say '..turn me inside out, make my heart speak..' I tried to remember a time when I felt that way. The only person I could think of was Lance- the Architect/hustler that broke my heart into a thousand pieces and never came back to mend it. I felt my eyes watering and tried to shake the thought of that tired negro from my head. I felt myself breaking into a full fledged cry. Not over Lance, just life period. I kept seeing different episodes of my life where I felt used, lonely, or just unworthy. I reached down and clicked the radio off. Tried to click away the memories. The rest of the drive was in silence.

Once home, I throw on some old, worn out jeans and my red and white sorority t-shirt. I want to be comfortable at the movies. I pull my hair back with a white scrunchie and headed out the door to go pick up Sharon.

I took the 295 to Sharon's apartment in Orange Park. Why she felt the need to live out in the boonies is beyond me. When I finally arrive at her complex, she is standing outside holding her purse and looking at her watch as if I'm making her late for her own wedding or something. I roll down my window.

"Hey girrrrl. I'm sorry I'm running late. It's takes foreva to get out here."

"Whatever." She said as she slammed my car door and adjusted her seat. "And why you up in here looking like the queen of grunge?" She asked while struggling with her seatbelt.

"Kiss what I twist, knucklehead, I ain't dressing up just to chill with your funky butt."

"Alright, Gina. You gon' miss your Denzel one day walking around looking like broke Bonita-

and what happened with you and Sean? You always get like this when y'all have a blow-up."

Arrrgggh. I hate the fact that she can always tell what's up with me. I ignore her question and pretend to adjust my sun visor.

"There ain't no sun out, G." She says as she slams the visor back up. "I know you heard my question."

"Nothing Sharon."
She didn't respond. She sat back in her seat and waited for me to tell her. This was our way.

"He has a girlfriend---and she heard Sean and I having sex over his cell phone." I was too ashamed to tell her the whole truth.

"What?" Her eyes popped. "How?"

"I'oun know," I lie, "I guess we must've rolled over on the phone."

"Damn. That's messed up. You surprised?"

"Not really. I suspected he had somebody. She thinks she's the one, too."

"Well didn't you think you were the one?"

I hit the brakes and contemplate doing a u-turn and dropping her ass right back off where I got her from. I decide against that and ignore her the rest of the way to the theatre.

We go inside and head straight to the concession stand, our usual routine. The skinny heifer with the burgundy vest behind the counter was so rude. She just stood there, looking at us like 'what?'. We ordered popcorn, nachos, Raisinettes, Mike Ikes, and cherry slushees. I hate when Sharon eats Raisinettes though. Those things make your teeth look like nasty cavities. The concession stand attendant rolled her eyes and handed us our food. I smiled and thanked her anyway. I was tempted to hand her a card to go see Donatello, my hair stylist, because her French roll is tore up and played out.

"What was her problem?" I ask Sharon as we walk away.

"Her taps are probably hurting her."

"Her what?"

"Taps. T.A.P. Tight ass pants."

We both burst out into laughter as we round the corner into the dark theatre showing *Why Did I Get Married.*. We must've been louder than we thought because the only people in there, an interracial couple-black man, white woman-looked at us as if we had committed a horrible crime just by showing up. The man shook his head as if he was disappointed that we had walked in. When we walked past them, the woman placed a concentrated gaze on her man and did not blink once. It is always hilarious to see how intimidated our usually bold white counterparts get when they are afraid their men might look at us and get homesick.

"Honey, she is safe." I whisper to Sharon laughing. "He look like a broke ass Snoop Dogg."

"I know, right?"

The man kept his hen-pecked eyes glued to the screen, daring not to look our way. We sat about 7 or 8 rows in front of them. The movie was pretty good. I had to nudge Sharon a couple of times to ask her to stop smacking those Raisinettes so loud. She gets on my nerves. Tyler Perry is such a good writer. I am so relieved not to see him playing Madea in this one though. He plays the part a little too well sometimes.

On the way out of the theatre, Sharon and I cracked up when white woman/black man got to the lobby where we could see them in the light. She had on a pair of Levi's that had to be one of the first makes. They were cutting up her ass so bad that I felt sorry for the inner seam. Plus, they were high waters and she had on a dingy beige blouse and get this—white pumps. I normally don't laugh at people's clothes, but it was too funny considering that the man was very well dressed in a pair of black slacks, a charcoal grey shirt, and a nice leather belt and shoes to match. None of that helped the fact that he was ugly as sin, but I couldn't help but to wonder if he would have tolerated such a tacky looking black woman. Doubtful. I wonder why that is.

Outside in the parking lot, Sharon and I were walking to the car when Sharon stopped dead in her tracks and froze like she had seen a ghost.

"Whuz wrong wit'chu?" I ask looking around to see if she had witnessed a crime or something. I didn't see anything. "Sharon, wh…"

"Shhhh," she cut me off. "Listen…" She looked like she was trying to connect with a spirit that I couldn't see.

"I know that voice anywhere," she continued while ducking behind a dusty blue Buick LeSabre. I don't know why, but I ducked with her. "that's Michael, his voice is coming from that Durango over there."

"You tripping." I say emphatically and stand from my crouching position. Sharon grabs my arm and pulls me back down.

"Trust me Gina. I'm gon' bust his ass this time. Come on."
I tried to grab her shoulder to keep her from making a giant ass of herself, but she snatched away and took off toward the Durango. She was ducking behind cars and in and out of spaces like a ninja. The whole time I was right behind her, ducking and

sliding too, hoping nobody would see us and think we were stalkers. When we were about 10 feet from that black Durango, Sharon stopped again and looked like she was connecting to that invisible spirit again.

"What?" I whisper while wiping sweat from my forehead with my palm."

"Yeah, that's him." And with that, Sharon stood up and was upon the Durango in one pounce. She beat on the passenger side window hard two times and I saw the man and woman inside jump. The whole truck shook.

"Get out Muthafucka. Get the fuck out the truck."
Oh lord. I thought she was going to handle this without a scene. I should have known better. The whole parking lot froze. A few ignorant people moved closer to get a better look. I slowly backed away and tried to look uninvolved. But if it comes to blows, I know I will have to get involved. That's my dawg.

Michael eased the window down a little bit. "Stop beating on this window crazy ass bitch. You following me?"

"You sorry bastard," she kept yelling, "get out the car 'fo I bust these windows!"

I hear the woman inside the truck call Michael a muthafucka and tell him to get out before that crazy ho breaks her windows. I laughed at that one. Michael finally got out looking scared. He double jumped when he looked in the cut and saw me standing between a Dodge Caravan and a Miata. Good. Now he knows not to put his hands on her.

"Why are you following me?" Michael asked Sharon trying to sound calm, maybe in attempt to disperse the crowd.

"Who is she?" Sharon asks, pointing at the lady in the truck.

"Don't worry about who the fuck I'm with. I ain't married to you. I ain't gotta answer to your stupid ass."

Sharon's lip started to quiver like she was going to cry. She tries to play the hard role, but I know it hurts like hell when the man you love treats you like that. I know. Especially if he does it in front of the other woman.

Michael continued his rant. "You too clingy Sharon. Stop following me and my lady around. We ain't together no more."

Sharon looked as if those words stabbed her like a knife. She opened her mouth but no words came. Michael turned around and pulled on the door handle to get back in the truck. It was locked. He tapped on the window. It took him a couple of seconds to realize that the woman had intentionally locked his slow ass out. He looked stupid standing there with his hand on the door handle begging her to open the door. The lady opened the passenger side window just enough for her to talk to him. She was loud. Very loud.

"What kind of fool do I look like? Huh?" Mystery lady demanded.

"Baby let me explain…" Michael begged.

"Explain what nigga? That I should let this go so you can do the same thing to me? Disrespect me in front of a parking lot full of people, call me a bitch and leave with the other woman? Naw my brother. You got it wrong. If yo' punk ass will disrespect one woman, you'll do it to another one. I ain't no young fool." With that, she looked toward me and Sharon. "Y'all ladies alright?"

"Uh, yeah." Sharon managed. I just nodded yes.

"Y'all have a good evening." She started up her truck and pulled off. Then stopped and yelled back at us. "And don't give his punk ass a ride home."
We both laughed. Sharon picked up her black mules, which she had kicked off when she was ready to open up a can of whoop ass on Michael. We walked back to my car. Friends. With familiar hearts.

Illusion

My sister Monica and I had been planning Sharon's surprise birthday party for months. We had done a great job of keeping it a secret. That is, until I made the mistake of telling one of her ghetto cousins who immediately called Sharon up and asked her what kind liquor would be served. It was no longer a surprise party, but nevertheless, we were all very excited about it. We needed to cut loose.

The day of the party I was a nervous wreck. I don't know why, I guess because we had invited so many people and made such a big "to do" about it, we wanted to make sure the party lived up to everybody's expectations.

I walked around the clubhouse we had rented and gave it a once over. It looked nice. We had strategically placed food stations and very few chairs around the room. A party book I'd read said that this set up would encourage people to mingle more. There was a sushi station, my idea. We kept the choices simple: California rolls, Philadelphia rolls, and Spicy Tuna rolls. At an angle near the large bay window that overlooked a lake was a pasta station-with a real pasta chef. Well, really it was my cousin Richard, but he had taken a culinary class over the internet while he was in the county jail. So technically, at least in my mind, he was a chef. I'd promised him 20 bucks and a 12 pack of Bud if he'd do the job. Of course I didn't pay him in advance because he probably wouldn't have shown up. We also had a meats and cheeses station, to which we had to add deviled eggs after Sharon found out about the party.

I straightened the marble slab with the wheel of Brie on it and looked around once more. The red candles cast a gorgeous orange glow and plumeria smell throughout the room. The wine bar was stocked with wine, champagne and glasses galore. All the wine was inexpensive, but we sat the bottles in pretty wine straw baskets to hide the Riunite and Andre labels. The party would be starting in an hour, I needed to go and get dressed. On the way, I passed through the kitchen and found my cousin Richard rambling through one of the drawers. I hoped he was not stealing these people's stuff. The clubhouse was on my credit card.

"What'chu doing Richard?"

"Looking for a big knife." Oh lord. He's going to cut somebody.

"For what?" I asked hoping the Deejay or somebody hadn't pissed him off.

"To cut up my tomatoes for the pasta bar, cuz. Relax." He cut me a grin.

"Oh." Whew. "Alright Richard. Be cool tonight man. Be cool."

He knew what I meant. We've always connected like that. We could get along and I never judged him, despite his poor decisions that kept landing him in jail.

"You got it cuz." His smile and flashed all thirty-two goldies at me as I left to go home and get dressed for the party.

Once I make it down the I-95 to Southside boulevard to Tinseltown, I slow down and make peace with being late tonight. Being fashionably late doesn't really count as late anyway. I go into the apartment and light candles everywhere-so I can feel sensual as I get dressed. I run my big blue tub full of warm water and dump a half a box of Epsom salts in to ease the swelling in my ankles. I retain water like a mug sometimes. I sit down in the water and turn my focus to God.

"Thank you.." I talked to God and thanked Her for the opportunity to be alive. I asked Her to let me party tonight until the sun comes up. She understands.

I put on my red dress with the dip so low in the back that crack almost kills. I look in the mirror and shock myself. I didn't even know I could look this damn good. My red strappies are five inches. These are the ones that usually never touch the floor. By the time I finish applying my Mac, Clinique, Black Opal, and everything else I can find, I hear a knock at the door. It's Sharon. I peep at her through the peephole and asks her "who is it?" anyway.

"Open the damn door. I saw your big eye looking at me through the peep hole."
I giggle and open the door. Sharon looks pretty. She is wearing a long, flowing, t-strap black dress with a split the goes clean up to her split.

"Dang girl. You tryna 'catch' tonight huh?" I tease her.

"Yep, you too, huh?"

"Damn right. Damn muthafucking right." I say as I go grab my purse, keys and a little moisturizer to put over my make-up. I don't like that embalmed look.

I let Sharon drive because secretly I had an agenda of my own. I'd invited my ex, Kiah, down to the party, and I don't think I'll be leaving alone tonight. We still get down like that from time to time. It was our unspoken code.

"What you smirkin' about?" Sharon snapped me out of gaze.

"Nothing. Just going over my grocery list in my head."

"Whateva heffa," Sharon said staring at me. She knew something was up.

"Light's green trick. Go."

When we get to the party, it's still early, but Sharon's ghetto friends are there waiting in line at the door, like its ladies night at the club. I can already hear the music pumping from inside, so I know the Deejay is on point. Once inside, Sharon heads straight for the wine bar, stopping to acknowledge people's "happy birthday" wishes. I follow her; maybe a drink will calm my nerves. I'm still thinking about Kiah. He's my homeboy, but I know tonight will be one of our "on" nights, where we become more than that for a few hours. I think my nervousness is actually excitement. After getting my white wine and downing it in one gulp. I go to the bathroom to pee out my anxiety. I pass by Sharon's gift table, which already has a few boxes and gift bags on it.

By the time I come out of the restroom, my wine has kicked in and more people are arriving. I feel mellow and sexy. It could be the wine, or it could be this lacy panties and bra set I got from sister Victoria. Either way, I feel sexy and excited, so Kiah will definitely be reaping the benefits.

I squint in the dim lights to see my watch. 10pm. Where's Kiah? I know his flight landed time because I called to check three times. It landed at 5:57pm. I was on my way to the kitchen area to call his cell phone when I see Kender, one of my coworkers. Kender grabs my arm and pulls me to the dance floor. Ken was a fad. F.A.D. Fine and doggish. He was wearing the hell out of that suit though. If I didn't know any better... But I do. He has been through every sister who doesn't know any better at the television station. I even heard he had a stint with Marilyn, the company asshole. Trifling. But tonight it doesn't matter, we're just dancing. The deejay switches it up and puts on "Set if off"- the black folks anthem. Everybody heads to the floor to do the bus stop-wait, I recently learned that that's a South Georgia term only- I meant the electric slide. My cousin Tara is the designated "bus stop caller". She hollers out whether we need to dip, double dip, drop, etc. We are rolling with laughter and sweating. Just as I am coming up from my 'double dip' the clubhouse door opens and Kiah walks in. I am so happy. Now, when the party is over I can tell him all about what happened with Sean, get snot all over his shirt while I cry it out, and listen to him tell me "I told you so" while I get my boots knocked to Timbuktu.

      I head his way so I can pull him to the dance floor. When I get about 3 steps away from him, the clubhouse door opens again and he looks back. In walks some hoochie mama with a short black dress on. It must be one of Sharon's ghetto friends, because her heels are higher than mine. Kiah waits for the girl to catch up with him and suddenly I become Beyonce and lose my breath. I know he did not do this. He did not bring somebody to my best friends birthday party. She catches up to him and hooks her arm through his. Yep. He brought her. It's too late for me to turn around a walk away without being obvious, so I continue toward him at a snails pace. Two steps are two miles now. I go ahead and hug him. As I do, my eyes meet hers. She looks me up and down, so I return the favor. As soon as I let him go, she flipped mode and started acting all sweet.

"I'm glad you made it." I told Kiah, giving him a 'you know you're wrong' look.

"Hey Gina. Ahh. This is Leslie. Leslie, Gina."

"Charmed." I couldn't even fake it. I know I was being catty, but Kiah knows better than this. I know he's not my man, but like I said, we have an unspoken code. I feel so stupid to be crushed over this, but I am.

"Y'all, make yourselves at home. Have some drinks," I tell them. "Kiah, we got that pasta you like."

"Cool Gina. Save a dance for me," he said as he and Ms. Six inch heels Leslie walk off into the crowd.

"Save a dance for me." I mimic while walking off the other way. There goes my night. Sharon must've caught my pitiful face as I headed to the bathroom, because she followed me there.

"What's wrong?" She sang. She was drunk already. "Don't cry, pretty." Really drunk.

"Sharon, Kiah brought a girl with him. Can you believe that?"

"Was she mean to you?"

Why am I talking to her right now?

"Never mind," I say, forcing myself to pull it together. "I'm cool." I put a couple of Bausch and Lomb moisture drops in my eyes and head back into the party. Kiah is waiting for me at the bathroom door.

"What was that about Gina?"

"Why did you bring her?" I didn't even try to fake it.

"Gina, I thought you would be kicking it with Sean."

"I wouldn't have invited you if Sean was coming." That came out wrong.

"Oh it's like that," he sounded offended. "I'm your backup?"

"I didn't mean it like that Kiah, but you know how we kick it when you come to town." I look down at his flashy gators to keep from making eye contact with him. I laugh when I see them. He knows what I am laughing at and laughs too. Then shoots me a bird. I shoot back and continue. "Why you played me like that, Kiah?"

"Gina, I gotta have a life too. You always telling me about this man and that man. What am I s'pose to do?"

He had a point. But I'm not feeling rational right now. I'm emotional.

"Whatever." I say walking off.
He knew where I was coming from. The discussion was over, but we both knew that we had understood each others points. I danced with Kiah a couple of times and tried to grind up on him real close to see if I could get him excited. I could.

He whispered in my ear, "Don't do that, Gina. Leslie's here."
That made me grind even harder. When the song was over, I saw her looking me up and down. I knew I was half wrong. But he used to be my man so I was also half right. I have to go home alone tonight, but my night does not have to be totally dry.

By the time I finished grinding my ass and grinding my teeth on some pasta and sushi, it was three a.m. and I was tired as a mug and ready to go home. My stupid ass didn't have a ride home though, because Sharon was drunk and headed home with Kender. Kiah is gone to bang Leslie's high heels off. I know I can't drive Sharon's car. Since my brother died, I don't play drinking and driving. At all.

I was standing in the half lit parking lot like a super-dummy asking to be robbed, when a hand on my shoulder scared the shit out of me. It was Leslie.

"Need a lift?" She looked sincere. "It's dangerous to be standing out here like this."

"Yeah, I didn't drive my car and my ride is tipsy."

"You can ride with me and Kiah." No she didn't say that like they are a couple or something. Getting your back banged out is one thing, but don't be saying 'me and Kiah'. Heffa.

Once inside the car, I sat in the backseat and pretended to be sleeping so I could eavesdrop on Kiah and Leslie's conversation. To my surprise, it was silent most of the way. Kiah is a big talker. He must really like this girl. Either that or he felt uncomfortable with the two of us in the car together.

As we approach the IHOP on Atlantic Boulevard, he asks Leslie if she's hungry. She says yes, and then he hollers to the back seat of this cheesy rental car to ask if I'm hungry. I'm not. I lie and say yes just to be a fly on the wall.

The IHOP at 4 a.m. is like the 1a.m. at the club- packed as hell. We finally get a table next to what I assume are a group of college students, probably just leaving the club. They are loud and obnoxious. Leslie and Kiah sit on one side of the table, which leaves me sitting on the other side hiding behind a menu looking like the third wheel loser that I am. Our waitress takes or drink orders while Kiah stares at her size DDD breasts. I'm secretly glad that he's gawking because Leslie notices and readjusts herself in her chair to grab his attention. He looks embarrassed. After Leslie orders a Fajita Omelet, my favorite-this heifer has my man and my omelet-she got up and excused herself to the restroom. I order a Veggie Omelet because I'll be damned if I make the hoochie think I want to be like her. When Leslie disappears around the corner, Kiah sneers at me.

"Why didn't you order the Fajita omelet?" He reads me even better than Sharon does. He already knows why I didn't order the damn omelet.

"Why did you order that steak? You know you can't afford it, plus it's gon' aggravate your hemorrhoids."

He shoots me a bird and continues taunting me. "What'chu doing tonight Gina?"

"Whatever Kiah," I knew what he was getting at. "You might be doing her but you'll be thinking about me." I say and then laugh.
His eyes suddenly become serious and he doesn't blink or respond.

Ms. Six inch heels returns from the restroom with a fresh coat of berry colored lip gloss and a fresh spray of some cheap perfume. It smells like Sand and Sable. I know because I used to wear it in high school. Now that I think about it, scent association is probably while Kiah is attracted to her anyway. I coughed a little to over emphasize the fact that I smelled it. He shot me a 'behave' look.

We ate in awkward silence for I little while until I finally spoke up.

"So...Leslie, what do you do?"

"I'm a hairdresser."

"Really?" I faked interest and thought to myself that maybe she needs to hook her own hair up. Her little '92 Halle Berry cut is a bit played. "Are you a barber too? Kiah needs somebody to hook that neck up," I joked.

"That's alright baby," she says looking a Kiah and rubbing his head, "I like that neck."

"Well break out the bubbly." Oops. Didn't mean to say that out loud.

"So I hear you work at a radio station Gina." She says to me.

"Television station." I corrected her. Bitch.

"Sounds exciting."

"It's a living." I reach for the check. "Y'all ready?"

"I got that." Kiah cut in taking the check from me.

"Showing off?" I smiled.
He let that one go. Leslie got up and walked toward the register and I got up and walked behind her. Kiah put a 5 dollar tip on the table and trotted up behind me and grabbed my ass. This is a game we've played since high school. I discreetly reach behind me and give his crotch a squeeze. As soon as I look up, I catch Leslie's eyes on me in the big wall mirror behind the cash register. Busted. Kiah saw her too, and we both approached the register silently, like two kids on the way to the principal's office. Kiah seemed scared, but I was like-whatever. I'll do the explaining. When we get a few feet from her, she turns and walks out the door and goes outside. Kiah pays the bill and I wait for him.

"I guess you're in trouble." I say as he holds the door open for me.

"My mama's in Georgia." He says trying to play it cool.

"But your woman's over there by the car." I say matter-of-factly.

Leslie turns her back to us and faces the door of the rented Nissan Altima as we approach her. Kiah grabs my ass again. I laugh out loud at his stupidity. Ole girl must've thought I was laughing at her because she snapped.

"Oh it's funny huh? I'm a joke?" She turns from me to Kiah. "Am I a joke Kiah?"

"Get in the car Leslie," he responds. She does.

I sat in the backseat in silence, hoping they wouldn't argue. Not because I care about this stupid issue, but because I know Kiah makes the best love after an argument. I'm jealous that it won't be me. That's wrong, but true.

Out of the blue, Leslie says "Take me to the airport."

"Shut up." Kiah scowled.

Kiah was being mean and unnecessarily cruel. I guess he was trying to show off for me. That wasn't cool. I decided to speak up.

"That's unnecessary Kiah. Chill." She had a right to be mad. Hell, I would've been too.

"Oh, don't take my side now," she says to me. "You were the one grabbing his privates." Who says 'privates' anymore? I smiled.

"Look Leslie," I start explaining, "It's a stupid game we play and…"

She cut me off. "Well play this, if you want him that much that you have to be a slut in public. Have him"

I was silent for a minute. Then totally ignored her and leaned toward Kiah in the front seat.

"Kiah, take her ass to the airport like she asked you."

"Gina," he turned on me. "Don't do this shit tonight. Not tonight. I'm too tired for this."

Silence for the rest of the ride down Southside Boulevard. I felt like I should apologize but my pride wouldn't let me. When we get to my apartment, I mumble thanks and get out. Kiah didn't even wait to see that I got in the door safely. He pulled off as soon as my feet touched the ground. Bastard.

I walk into the apartment and don't even bother to turn the lights on. I go straight to the bedroom and plop across my bed. Why is my life a constant T.V. drama? It must be me. There is no way that everyone I come in contact with could be problematic. Oddly enough, this whole mess with Kiah made me miss Sean. How stupid. Why can't I care about somebody who cares about me too? I stand up from the bed and click the lamp on. I look in the full length mirror on the outside of the bathroom door. I do not like what I see. I see someone who is too dependent on other people for validation. As much as I want to be Ms. Independent woman, my personal life is anything but that. Even so, I wanted to call Sean. Yes, even after finding out about Ms.Hometown/diamond bracelet/thing. The red glow on the nightstand said for me to take my black ass to sleep, it is 5:45a.m. But that jittery feeling in my stomach says to stay awake. My body is probably getting a second wind.

I absentmindedly wander to the kitchen and open the fridge. I reach for the orange juice and knock over a half-empty can of Diet Cherry Coke. I get so clumsy when I'm upset. I roll off a half a roll of paper towels, drop it on the sticky mess, and leave it.

I peel off what was supposed to be my "Knock Kiah dead Red dress" as I head back to the bedroom. I drop it on the floor on the way. I crawl into bed under the comforter only.

I must've drifted off to sleep, because the phone was now waking me up. It was 9:00a.m. I didn't even look at the caller I.D. I knew it was Kiah.

"Hello."

"Hey."

"Hey."

"What's up?" he tried to play like nothing had happened.

"Nothing." I played too.

"Our flight leaves at 4:00, if I don't hit you before then, I'll hit you when we land."

He's still with the heifer. He didn't take her to the airport and leave her without waiting like he did me. She probably still gave him some too. Stupid trick. Still, I will not let him know I'm upset.

"Alright, Kiah. Y'all be safe." Click. I hang up without giving him a chance to respond. Damn him.

I jump out of bed and decide not to make it up. I just pull the comforter up over the rumpled sheets. My place is a mess. I will clean it later, I need to go workout right now. Work off some steam.

I change from my frilly red panties and bra and put on the heavy duty cotton stuff. You know, the three to a pack whities that keep you yeast infection free. I throw on an old, wrinkled Bob Marley t-shirt from the bottom of my drawer, then take it off because it reminds me too much of Lance. I grab a plain white Hanes tee-whoever decided to make these things tag-less is a genius.

Those tags itch like hell when you sweat. I pull on my grey tights, grab a face towel, and head out the door determined to make something of the remainder of my Saturday.

On the drive to Bailey's gym, I let the window down and let the dry, hot, Florida air blow on my face. Trying to get some clarity on my life. I flip on the radio and hear Alicia Keys telling some dude to hold her like it is the last time. I bob my head to the rhythm until a bump in the road makes me lose me beat. I look in the rearview and to both sides to see if I hit something. Nothing. Then I hear an awful bumpity bump bump noise. Damn. A flat. I look up to the sky and ask "why?" I pull my dirty Mustang to the shoulder and reach for my purse to get my cell. Dang-de-dang dang. I always leave my purse and cell at home when I go to the gym. Them skinny heifers steal like there's no tomorrow. Monique was right-skinny women are evil.

I get out of the car to examine the tire. Flat as a pancake. The good thing is I know how to change a tire. My ex-boyfriend Lance was a good-for-nothing cheater that treated me like shit, but at least the bastard taught me how to change a flat.

I pop the trunk to get my jack and spare. While bending over to lift out the tire, some jackass passed by and yelled, "damn, that's a big booty." I didn't even look up. The brother could have stopped to help.

"I can do this." I say to myself out loud trying not to get emotional. I play the process of changing a flat over in my head before I start. As I finish setting the jack up , I hear a car pull up behind mine. I look up and around. It's a green truck, the sun is glaring off the windshield, so I can't see the person inside. Quick Prayer: *Lord*

Please, No Jeffery Dahmer, No Charles Manson, No D.C. Sniper. Amen.

The door opens and a brother with a teeny weeny afro steps out. His skin is the color of chocolate milk. Shaken, not stirred.

"Need some help?" He says while already rolling up his sleeves.

"Yes, could you please call triple A for me? I left my cell at home."

He chuckles. Ain't nothing funny. I hope he's not about to go psycho on me.

"Would you believe I left my cell at home too? I was on my way back to get it when I saw you."

I rolled my eyes at his weak attempt at some game. I guess now I'm supposed to ask him to help me change the tire. Well he's wrong, I'm not going to ask him to help me. Oh forget it... To hell with women's lib.

I hand him the lug wrench and step further back onto the shoulder.   I look at him and wonder why he's wearing a dress shirt on a Saturday morning. He has a nice body. Doesn't look like he works out necessarily, but it does look like he works hard. He jacks up the car with ease and looks over at me.

"I'm Perry, by the way."

"Nice to meet you Perry. I'm Gina. Look I really appreciate..."

"Don't mention it. I would want someone to stop for my sister. If I had one."

I continued to size him up. He was shorter than I like them, but taller than me. Nice Goatee. Easy on the eyes.

"Did you hit something in the road?" He startles me.

"Huh? Oh, no. I don't think so. I didn't see anything."

"Yeah. Stuff happens sometimes."

"Tell me about it." I mumble.

I go back to watching Perry work. I like the way his hands, which were noticeably ringless, moved the tools with ease. He was barely breaking a sweat. I was drenched just watching.

"Well, that should do it." He says, dusting off his hands. "You might still want to go get your tires checked, balanced, all that good stuff."

"Thank you sooo much," I sing as I open the passenger door and take my emergency 20 dollar bill from the glove box. "This is for your trouble."

"No trouble," he pushes the twenty away. "Glad I could help. You take care, okay?"

"Oh…You too. Thanks again." I can't believe he didn't take the money. And he's really walking away. He didn't even ask for my phone number. I'm so impressed, I almost give it to him anyway.

I wave to Perry in the side mirror as I pull onto the road way. He waves back.

"He was sooo nice." I say to myself.

I pull into a gas station a few miles up the road. To my surprise, Perry pulls in right beside me in his F-150 super-cab. That green really is an ugly color.

I guess Perry saw the surprised look on my face. He put both hands in the air like I was the police and gave me a huge smile that revealed his deep dimples.

"I'm not a stalker Gina," he says out his rolled down window. "I'm sorry if I appear that way, but I wanted to ask you something."

I knew it. Here it comes. He wants my number.

"I was thinking," he continued, "would you like to come to my church tomorrow?"

I laughed. I didn't mean to, but that explains his nice-ness. He's a church boy. I've always shyed away from church boys. I know that sounds bad, but they usually seem nerdy.

"Okay. Ummm." How was I supposed to respond? "O—okay, I might do that. Where's the church?"

"Actually not too far from here. Joy For Life Ministries on Swelcher street."

"Oh, I know where that is. A couple of blocks down from the Publix—huge church on the corner."

"Yes, that's it. Should I expect to see you there?"

"Okay, I'll see what I can do."

He looked disappointed. I know that sounded too much like a *no*. I didn't want to say yes, because he'd end up sitting there doing a Bob Marley. Waiting in vain.

Realization

I surprised myself by arriving at the church at 10:15 on the dot. I wore my canary yellow Sag Harbor suit with the black and gold buttons. I stood in the huge foyer and looked at all the sisters and brothers filing into the sanctuary. Little girls with ponytails, ribbons, and ruffled socks held onto their mothers dress tails. The women out-numbered the men by far. I guess the church was no different than the rest of the world.

I found myself fidgeting with my straw bag just to keep my hands busy. I had left my bible at home on purpose, so Perry wouldn't see me struggling when it's time to find the scripture. I followed an elderly couple into the church sanctuary. It was even larger inside than it appeared from the street. I chose an aisle seat near the back entrance. I wanted to make it easy for Perry to spot me. The music started and everyone stood to their feet, so I followed suit. I kept door-watching for Perry. I hoped he hadn't stood me up. Being stood up at church would definitely be a first for me.

Five ladies and three men walked onto the platform with microphones, each one with a different color mic cover. They began singing and waving their hands. They looked really happy to be there. About two minutes into "Jesus is a rock", the preachers walk in from a side door to the pulpit. I look around at the door, still no Perry. I turn back around and see the fourth preacher come in and kneel in front of the big chair in the middle to pray. I chuckled with disbelief. It was Perry.

I looked down at the Order-of-Service program the white-gloved usher had handed me at the door. The front of it read: Joy For Life

Ministries. Perry G. Tyson, Senior Pastor, I almost
fainted.

MTB?

"Girrrrrl, he was da preacher?" Sharon asked in a pitch so high I had to pull the phone away from my ear.

"Yes girl, the *pastor*."

"You know God is tryna tell you something. You got Pastors Hollerin' at'cha."

"I know, right? Girl I made a break for the door as soon as he closed his little bible at the end of the sermon. I don't know if he really wanted to see me, or if he thought I was a sinner who needed savin'."

Sharon howled with laughter. "But for real Gina, could he preach?"

"Girrrl. He had little old ladies doing the c-walk and everything." I was joking with Sharon, but inside I was really intimidated. I had never even talked face to face with a preacher. Unless you count Kiah's mom ex-boyfriend who used to pray that he could 'lay hands' on her when Kiah was out of the house.

Getting through work the next day was not easy. I could not concentrate worth Jack. I kept taking the program from my purse staring at the church phone number. Why? I wasn't really feeling the brother like that. I guess curiosity was getting the best of me. What would it be like to date a preacher? He must be a powerful man having such a huge following of church members. Maybe I should call. I'll just leave a little message at his office. Scratch that. His secretary might get it and think I'm a hussy. Does he even have a secretary? I could call his home number. He had caught up with me in the church parking lot, patted me on the shoulder, and held my right hand as if we were discussing the sermon like the deaconesses do after church. He had slipped me a card that had his home number written on the back and asked me to call him later. I'd tucked it away in my purse and agreed, but I really had no intentions of calling him. True enough, this man was passably handsome and very kind, but he was a man of the cloth. What would he really think of me when he found out how much I loved cosmopolitans, R&B music, and a good lay. All on the same day. He would surely cast me out.

I checked the time on my computer screen-4:45pm. Thank you Jesus. I need to get out of here today. I need a mani and a pedi, and a drink. Well, skip the drink, gotta learn how to be the preacher's wifey. Why do women do that? Before the brother can open the door for us, we've already pictured him as the groom, the father of our twins, and the old man next to us on the porch in the rocking chair of the rest home.

On the way home from the station, I drove by the church-you know, just to see what I could see. I drove by quickly at first, worrying that he would spot my car and think I'm sweating him. After I saw that no one was standing around the church and there were only a few cars, none of which were green F-150s, I drove past again more slowly. I can't lie I was impressed that a man as young as Perry-how old was he anyway, he looked quite young-could run a church so large. He must be very driven. I find that so sexy. How could I be feeling like this? I took one last look at the huge stucco church while imagining myself stepping out of a pearlescent Cadillac with a wide brimmed "Sunday Hat" on, after having parked in the imaginary parking spot marked "First Lady".

"I think I'm going to call him," I say to no one. "Yep, I can do this."

At home that night I must've picked up that darn business card a million times and put it down again. I felt so nervous. Finally, I counted to 10 quickly and dialed.

"Hello."

"Um, hi!" I sounded so stupid.

"Hi Gina. I'm glad you called."

How'd he know it was me? I know I dialed *67. I think I did anyway.

"Hi Pastor, I mean Perry, Pastor Perry." Okay I should just hang up now and try to disappear.

"Perry, Gina, you don't have to be formal. Listen, uhh, I didn't mean to surprise you like that on Sunday, but I really wanted you to show up. I hope I didn't upset you."

"No, not at all," I lied. He had me going in circles. "I enjoyed your sermon very much."

"I'm glad you did. I figured that would be the best way for me to tell you what I do. I also sell Real Estate though."

"Oh. Okay" I said. Conversation is something I never usually have a problem with. I'm tripping.

"Well Gina I won't beat around the bush. I think you are a very attractive young lady and I would love to take you out and get to know you better.

"That sounds good, Perry. I'd love to get to know you better as well. What do you like to do?" A thousand things run through my head in 10 seconds. I imagine that he likes to go to homeless shelters, pass out church leaflets, and visit the sick and shut in. What am I getting myself into?

"Well Gina, I'll leave it up to you. I'm game for whatever you want to do. How's Friday evening?"

"Friday's fine."

"7:30?"

"Yes, 7:30's okay with me." I give him my address and immediately start looking around the apartment for things I would have to hide when he comes over. Number one on the list, all those "cussing" movies my mama had warned me about watching anyway. She swears "Bad Boy's II" is satan's work. Boy, if I pull off a date with a preacher I will be henceforth truly known as the playa I dream to be. I hang up with Perry and start to take inventory of my life. I feel overwhelmed when I think about all the things I would be ashamed to share with him. Things I've said, done, thought. Wow. And he's just a man. Judgment day is going to be something serious.

Getting through the work day Friday was a black bear. I'm a serious list writer. I had three going at one time. First was a list of possible outfits, including shoes, accessories and make up. Next was my "to do" list. Shave my legs, do the last of my cleaning, plug up my vanilla Glade Plug Ins, etc. And lastly, questions I wanted to ask Perry. My girl Sharon had been helping me come up with things for us to do on this date. I had been careful to avoid venues where alcohol is served, cussing music is played, or dancing encouraged. Didn't want him to feel uncomfortable or think, i.e. know, I was a wild, loose woman. That meant most of the things I like to do was out. So I decided to keep it simple. We'd have dinner and then take a walk out at The Landing overlooking the St. John's river and listen to the live jazz band. I'd chosen Ari's in San Marco

as the restaurant. It was an African American
owned place with sort of Caribbean/Soul food
fusion going on. A lot of people in Jacksonville
were sleeping on Ari's. It's just something about us
that makes us not support our own. It's an upscale,
yet casual/metro environment with food that is out
of this world. The owner is always there, making
her rounds to greet customers, and bringing trays of
food for people to sample. If she was someplace up
north or out on the west coast, you know where we
are more likely to embrace our own culture, she'd
be a millionaire by now.

      I was a nervous wreck while sitting at home
waiting for Perry to pick me up. I'd worn the carpet
damn near bare pacing from the mirror to the
window. I kept checking to see if I needed to wear a
slip with my slinky dress. I hope not, because I
don't think I even own a slip. The only reason I
know what one is is because my mother made sure
my sister and I had white, black, and beige half and
whole slips for church and school. She wanted no
chance of our little silhouettes showing the little
piss tail boys what we were working with, which is
understandable because my whole family has been
bootylicious long before Beyonce' ever thought of
that word. The drape neck on my coral, flowy
sundress gave it a dressy look. It was one of those
dresses that can blend in with any setting. If he was
dressed up, I'd fit, and if he'd decided to go with
khaki's and a polo, I'd still fit. So I was happy
about that. I struggled for the longest with whether
or not to rock my 4 inch pumps, but I decided I had
to. They give my legs such a defined, sexy
appearance. Hell, I don't know how much preacher
he is, I'm I know I'm still a woman. And I don't

care how much bull shit I've been through, tonight
I'm still a rose.

The loud ass ringing phone shook me from
my Aretha Franklin moment. I buzzed Perry into
the gate and gave myself a once over in the mirror.
One last dab of Michael Kors on my wrists, ankles
and knees. Not that any of those places would be
getting attention tonight. I grabbed my clutch bag
and keys to meet him at the door. Although I'd
cleaned and hidden my sinner things thoroughly, I
still didn't want him to come in. I may have missed
a spot or something. I counted his footsteps and he
ascended the stairs. His steps seemed much more
relaxed and patient that Sean's ever had. As he
reached the top step I inhaled and blew out a long,
cool breath to relax. I waited a few seconds after he
knocked to swing the door open. I greeted him with
a warm smile and he stepped forward as if he was
going to come in. I stepped forward too and hugged
him instead. Immediate regret. Much too soon to be
pressing my breasts all up against the preacher man.
I know he thinks I'm a fast hussy.

"You look great, Gina, wow. Smell good
too."

"Thank you, you look pretty handsome
yourself. You ready to go?" I'm sure he figured out
that I didn't want him to come in.

"Mind if I use your restroom first?"

Damn.

"Sure. Right through my bedroom and to
your left."

Double damn. Did I put my silver bullet
back in its satin pouch? And please father don't let
him look in the bathroom cabinet and see my
flavored massage oil and warming KY liquid. As he
walked through my room, I hope he didn't have any

divine visions about the people who've been here and what they'd done here. This is a bit much. I went to the fridge and took a swig of the Riunite I'd hidden behind the strawberry lemonade. Straight from the bottle. I heard the toilet flush and scrambled back to the sofa. Smelling like Kors and Lambrusco. I'm so damn slow sometimes.

"Okay, Gina. I'm good to go."

"Alright Perry. Just let me powder my nose." I said headed to take a quick swig of my hot cinnamon Scope so he wouldn't know I'd had communion before Sunday.

I was so relieved upon reaching the parking lot to see that I didn't have to climb up in an F-150 in four inchers. He was driving a BMW 745li. Black. He better do the damn thang. Conversation flowed well on the ride to Ari's. He opened the door for me in the car and the restaurant. Even pulled out my chair. I was digging this brother more and more. I know fish is an aphrodisiac for me, but I threw caution to the wind and ordered the crème de coconut mahi-mahi. He ordered Spicy Shrimp with curried peanut sauce. Over dinner the way he looked at me made me feel exposed. He kept giving me a look that says, "I know." And I swear if I didn't know he was a preacher, the way he was licking his lips would have made me hand him my panties under the table. I really needed a glass of wine to calm the butterflies that were fluttering their wings on the backs of my knees.

"Perry." Oh I said that too airy. That sounded sexy.

"Yes, Gina." He caught it.

"How is it that you became a preacher?"

"Well... I guess that's sort of like me asking you how you became a woman. Some things are just meant to be."

Butterflies

Some things are just meant to be. That date became the first of many over the next couple of weeks. We saw movies, went bowling, even fishing…his idea. I don't think he'll ever ask me to do that again, after a fish he'd caught fluttered around in the cooler and startled me, which in turn made me stand up in the 12 foot boat, almost fall, catch myself, and then fall anyway. Overboard. With his keys. Which we never found. After that we pretty much stuck to non-nature activities. He eventually reprimanded me for picking kiddie movies and said that he's not too uptight to see regular movies. He even offered me a glass of wine the first time I visited his house. I shot him a look. His response was simple: *What was Jesus' first miracle?* He was right, I remember reading about the wedding at Cana. But this could have been a test. I declined the wine.

Now his house- this was a house if I'd ever seen one. Looked like something straight out of a magazine. Not too much décor, but not the empty, black and white, cold look that everybody on MTV Cribs went for. His living room was full of taupes, rusty oranges, forest greens and rich burgundies. It was simple, yet so warm and inviting. Must be that religious vibe. It was very masculine, but still looked like a woman probably helped him achieve that "masculine look".

"Have you ever been married, Perry?" I know that seemed out of the blue. There's a method to my madness.

"No, Gina," he said watching my eyes as I scrutinized his décor. "Ethan Allen decorated my

110

home." He added with a knowing smile. "Have you?"

"Who me? Oh, no. Nope. Single as the day I was born." I said as I walked toward his French doors that led the deck out back without him offering me to do so. He followed. His back yard was huge. Every kind of tree you could imagine made Perry's yard its home. Some so tall I couldn't see the top of them. I was so lost in the branches and leaves and colors and sounds that 3 or 4 minutes must have passed before I spoke.

"This is beautiful…I mean… Just gorgeous." I managed.

And adding to the splendor was the sun putting on a spectacular sky show for us. Red, purples, corals, and silver. We were both quiet. Just enjoying the moment. He must really be a preacher because I know I felt God's presence. He was right there looking at us.

All I could say was, "wow."
Then it happened. We were standing near the edge of the porch admiring the private art display that God was putting on for us, when he leaned in and kissed me. Not a peck. A deep, sensual kiss that made me step away and turn my back to him to catch my breath. Before I could pull myself together he was standing behind me putting his arms around my waist. He pulled me to him. He was hard. I jerked away fast and swung around to look at him like the fraud he was. He tried to comfort me be pulling me back to him and kissing my face.

"What are you doing?!" I all but yell at him looking him up and down. Mostly down.

"I'm a man, Ms. Gina. It's okay. I know I don't have to act on every feeling I get. That doesn't mean I don't get those feelings. It's really alright. I just wanted to kiss you sweetie. That's it. Sorry about... Um. Sorry."

I looked down at the tent in his pants and couldn't help but to laugh. I hope he didn't think I was laughing at him, but this situation was awkward as hell and quite funny.

"I'm sorry to act like that Perry. I just didn't know that preachers get...well, get.. you know."

"A hard on?" He said with an embarrassed look as he adjusted his crotch. "I'm really sorry."

Silence. Then we both crack up. I really felt a little better. At least now I know he's human. I don't have to feel so ashamed when he brushes against me and I feel a prickly heat come over me. That evening instead of going to dinner like we'd planned, we stayed at his house on the deck and talked about love, life, religion, philosophy, the future, children, babies, waterfalls, butterflies, and coral skies. Soon the same sun that put on fireworks display for us the evening before was waking and stretching before our eyes. Had we talked all night? Couldn't have. I remember too much silence. There were moments I guess when we had the sense to be quiet and let our spirits converse. We fell in love. Damn. Did I say love?

Sightless Wings

How could I let a preacher fall in love with me? I am being so selfish and unfair to him. He doesn't know the real Gina. He knows the Gina that talks gently and quietly and lets him get a word in edgewise. He doesn't know that I cuss like a sailor when I'm pissed off. He knows the kind Gina that turns the other cheek when someone does her wrong. He has no clue that I'm a professional Monday through Friday only. I will cut your ass on Saturday and pray for you to get better on Sunday. It's just my way. And I'm not about to change it just because I am in... well just because I like this man. So if he wants to try to hem me up into his little world, he can keep right on trying. He's no better than anybody else. Hell. He can be played just like the rest of them. He probably trying to play me anyway. How could he be a real preacher and offering somebody wine?

Rrring. Calling my girl Sharon.
        "Hello?"
        "Wake up Sharon, it's me. You up?"
        "Gina? You done lost your damn mind do you realize it's 5 o'clock in the..."
        I cut her off. "Sharon I'm in love." I couldn't even believe I was saying it. But it was true. I loved Perry. The preacher. Wow.
        "What? With who Gina? If you bout to say Sean I'm hanging up."
        "No silly," I laughed, "with Perry. He is soooo.... I don't know. He just is."
        "You tripping Gina. You are chha-ripping, hear me? You tripping."
        " I know," I sang. "And it feels so damn good."

"See, and you still cussing. How you in love with a preacher and you cussing. You have really bumped your head this time."

"Trust me Sharon," I said while rolling over in my new 700 count sheets which I couldn't afford, but had to have after I trashed all the other ones that Sean had put his body on, "I know I sound crazy, and I know I've said this a million times before about other guys. But this is just different, Share. I even feel him in my sleep."

"Gina did yall…"

"No crazy! I meant I feel his spirit. Oh, I'll call you back, he's calling."

"Bye nut."

"Hello?" I put on my cute morning voice as I clicked over to greet the love of my life.

"Morning sweetheart."

"Good morning, handsome." I blushed. This man made my black ass blush.

"I was hoping I could see you today. Maybe for breakfast."

"Well I'd love too, but you know I have to work, boo." Boo, I called him my boo. This feels so good.

"I won't keep you long. Can you tell them you'll be a little late? Meet me at *Bistro 12* downtown in an hour? Just want to see you this morning."

"Well…I am kind of hungry. Okay, see you in an hour."

Getting dressed was easy. I wanted to look good, but I didn't stress so much about what he'd approve of and such. The blouse I chose was pretty low cut. Hell, I wanted him to look. I put on my "skinny" slacks. They were of course black and made me look 10 pounds thinner. Took out my hard rollers pulled my loose, curly, tendrils back behind my ears. My 2 karat cz earrings were blinging like a mug. I used to tell people that Sean bought them for me and let them assume that they were real. Sean ain't never bought me nothing but a damn headache. And that was real as hell.

As soon as I walked in *Bistro 12* I spotted Perry. He looked so nice in his grey suit. Only a real man could rock pink pinstripes and look that good.

"Hi baby." I beam as he stands to pull out my chair for me. I felt a little underdressed standing beside him.

"Hi love. You look nice today," he lied. Three days before Sunday, at that.

"Thank you. You ain't too shabby yourself."

We ate fresh melon, turkey bacon, eggs, and coffee while people-watching and flirting with one another. When we had finished eating and Perry noticed me checking my watch, he asked if I wanted to skip work today. I told him no, I had too much to do. He told me he wished we could do this every day. Talk over breakfast, flirt with each other, and laugh at funny looking people. The waiter interrupted our conversation and dropped off the bill. I reached for it, but he held his hand up to me to stop, and reached into his pocket to pull out his wallet. Then he did something that I'd seen a million times; The I-forgot-my-wallet pat. I was about to be mad as hell. I can't believe he would pull this on me. To complete the act he even stood up and did the check-my-pants shake down. I smacked my teeth and reached for my purse. Loser. By the time I found my Visa debit card he was on the floor looking for his "wallet" underneath the chair. The old Gina would have busted him in the head and left. But I played it cool. I placed my card on the table without words. He got halfway up and looked at me. It hit me. Like a ton of bricks. Perry was on one knee, holding something that was reflecting ROY G. BIV. Every color in the spectrum. I couldn't breathe. People in the restaurant were awwwing and applauding. I couldn't breathe.

"Gina I told you I want have breakfast with you every morning. Go to sleep with you at night, and everything in between. Marry me."

Speak Gina. Say something. Wait, breathe first. Breathe. My thought were going a mile a minute. "Yes." I said it. And then again, and again. By then everyone in the restaurant were smiling and applauding, and the tears came. Boy did they. Then the thoughts came. What am I doing? I barely know this man. After pulling myself together long enough to call the station and tell them I wouldn't be in today. I posed that question to Perry.

"What are we doing? I mean, really. What do we know about each other? This is crazy. My mother, oh my God, my mother is going to flip, she's never even met you."

"Gina, I know it feels crazy. You don't think I feel it too? Just trust me. Trust yourself. Close your eyes and jump with me."

And I did.

Imagination

My mother flipped out on me at first when I delivered the news via phone that I was getting married. And then she called all my aunts, on both sides, and had them call and flip out on me too. My sister Monica was the most supportive, she told me just to trust my heart. Eventually my mom came around, especially when she found out he was a preacher. She started buying me all kinds of hats and handkerchiefs, and giving me advice on how to be a preacher's wife. I thought it was too funny, how would she know anything about that? The only time my daddy came to church was that time he thought the deacon was trying to get with mama on the sly. And that day he came ready to whup ass. When I told daddy I was getting married, all he said was that he'd have a talk with the "lil' nig" and tell him what he expects from him. And trust me, when he gets the chance, he will.

Sharon wigged out on me a little, but then said she was happy for me. And then when she thought about his-our house, cars, and church, she jumped up, high-fived me, and told me I'd hit the jackpot.

"Sharon, girl, this is love. I know you think I'm playing or just going with the flow, but trust me I wouldn't marry him if I didn't think I could change."

"What you need to change for, Gina?" Sharon asked shaking her head. "See that's what scares me about you and him. He loves you, true enough, but does he know the real you?"

I knew she was right. But I was serious about changing after I get married. I know I could live right. Sex was one of my vices, but that's "legal" with your husband. And Perry himself told me I could still drink wine. I can give up clubbing. My purpose for going was to find a man. I can do this. I'll plan the wedding, and everything will be fine.

"I got this, Share, okay? All I need is for you to be there for me. You're my maid of honor, if you don't support me, who can I count on?"

"Okay," she hesitated, "you're my girl, and whatever you do I got you. I got your back, G."

I had a 1996 Terry McMillan moment and exhaled. And for the first time, I really believed I could do this.

That feeling lasted only a fleeting moment. All hell broke loose in the church Sunday morning when Perry introduced me to the congregation as his fiancé before he began his sermon. When the words rolled off his lips, you could hear a pin drop. And a couple of hymnals too. I stood there in my pale pink suit trying to hold my fake smile. It was so fake that my lips started to tremble. I saw an old lady stand, hold up one finger, and exit the church. A younger woman with a short cropped hair cut and nine inch nails mouthed "she's not even a member" to someone in the choir. A couple of the sisters on the front pew just sat there with their mouths open looking like fly catchers. Finally one of the older ladies, maybe the mother of the church, broke out into song and headed toward the front of the church. She was clapping and singing: *"We all want to wish you welcome, welcome, welcome, we all want to wish you welcome, welcome to the house of the lord"*. A few others followed her reluctantly. I stood there received their handshakes and accepted their "honorary" membership to the church, as Perry had explained to me happens automatically when the preacher marries someone who is a non-member.

At dinner after church, I was quiet. Feeling really overwhelmed and out of my league. Perry sensed it, and he was quiet too. Probably having some reservations of his own. I looked mostly down at the collard greens, cornbread, barbequed chicken, and macaroni and cheese I'd prepared in his kitchen. From time to time I'd stare out the back window into the tall trees. He did the same.

"Perry I don't know about this." Silence. "And you no doubt feel the same way. Look, it's not to late to just.."

"Shhhh," he cut me off, "hush baby. It's okay. I know. Don't you think I've toiled with this as much as you? A Third of my congregation is threatening to leave. My boys call me crazy. But I don't care, all I want is you Gina. This isn't normal for me either, trust me. I feel crazy as all get out. Sometimes I can't even remember your birthday..."

My turn to cut him off "What do you mean you can't remember my birthday? Now that is just ridiculous, I remember y..."

"I'm just saying Gina. None of that matters. I love you. And I want to make love to you."

Did he say? Did.. I know I heard him wrong.

"What?"

"I want to make love to you. I haven't touched a woman since I became a preacher, that's been over 5 years. I've never had the desire to touch anyone as strongly as I want to right now."

"Perry is that why you want to marry me? For some ass?" Damn, I cussed. Damn.

He acted like he didn't even hear it. "No, baby, I want to marry you because I love you and I want to grow old with you."

"Oh, I see how it goes, you don't want to sin or whatever, so you know you gotta be married to get some. I see what this is about. Then you can divorce me and still be within the church realm." I know I sounded like a madwoman.

"Church realm?" He laughed at me. "Gina listen to yourself. To do that would be deceitful, which is a form of lying, which makes it a sin anyway. So no, I would not be within the *realm*."

I stood and pushed my chair back with my legs. It made that screeching noise that makes my skin crawls as it slid across the terra cotta colored ceramic floor.

"I'm done." I said throwing my napkin on to my plate.

He stood too and reached out to grab me. I pulled away. Left my plate on the table and went to get my purse from the living room sofa. He followed. When I got to the sofa I realized that I left my keys on the kitchen counter by the microwave. When I turned to go get them I was face to face with Perry. His breath smelled like barbeque. He put arms around my waist and tried to kiss me, I turned away, so he kissed me on my neck instead. I tried to push him away but my arms had no strength. His kisses made me so weak. He was so sexy in his little white tee and slacks. I tried to escape but my body had a mind of it's own, so I kissed him back. If I didn't know any better I'd have thought Perry was easing my skirt up. I looked down. He was. I back away. His eyes were low.

"What are you doing?" I say barely able to speak.

"You think I want to marry you just to make love to you. Let me prove you wrong. Let me make love to you right now and then I'll still marry you."

"Perry no, you are talking crazy. I'm not going to let you do that. You are the pastor of a church. No. I'm not letting you."

"Please." He begged, not really needing my permission because my skirt was already above my hips. He had those bedroom eyes focused on my white lace Victoria's Secret heart collection panties. This could not be happening. I quit resisting and led him to his bedroom by the hand. He walked as if his legs were lead, laboring the whole way. Probably having an internal fight against man and God, all within himself. When we got to the bedroom, I walked over to the double doors that led out to his balcony and closed the vertical blinds. He sat down on the bed and removed his shoes. He leaned back on the large, oak headboard and watched me. Saw what his imagination had probably seen a long time ago. I undressed for him. Slowly. Deliberately. When I was down to my bra and panties I walked over to him and pulled him up from the bed. He stood, rocking as if he would fall. I helped him take off his white tee, and then unbuckled his black leather belt. The leather was so soft and smooth that I had to linger on it for a minute. I ran my fingers over the silver chrome buckle and then slightly raked my nails over his abdomen. He had a very nice physique. Firm. Felt like a real man. The old Gina in me couldn't wait to see what he was working with, but the new Gina knew it was best to play the shy role in this situation. I turned away from him and turned the Beige and Brown comforter back. Before I could get in the bed, I heard the familiar sound of coins in a man's pocket jingling as his pants hit the floor. I turned and got a peek of his silk boxers and the tent that looked as if it could sleep a family of four. I pretended that I wasn't happy and anxious and looked away. We both slid under the covers and resumed what we'd started in the living room. He kissed me like there was no tomorrow. I felt him turn his body slightly so he could reach down and feel the fire. For the first time in my life, I was embarrassed that I was so wet. That told the story. Everything I was trying to hide was openly revealed. He knew I wanted him just like he wanted me. He slid a finger inside and I gasped. He looked in my eyes so intensely that it felt like he could see another part of the world through me. He leaned down and kissed my breast. I was so turned on by the little circular motions of his head and the warmness of his wet mouth, I was going to lose it. He moved to the other breast and I squirmed but he held me down, while now pleasuring me with two fingers. I was a river. And he was my current. I whispered in his ear "you got a condom?"

He shook his head no while still sucking so gently on my peaches. "I won't come inside. We don't need one."

With anybody else, I would have put up an argument, but Perry was going to be my husband, so I shared my diamond with him. In the rough. All the air escaped my lungs when he put it in. I wanted to shout. I'm talking bout church shout. He was big. The kind of big that you tell your friends about. He stretched my silk walls and I couldn't tell which way was up or down. My head was spinning. I felt him flip me over so he could get it from the back. Was this the same man that a few hours ago was preaching from the second chapter of Romans? He was hitting it so good that I wanted to tell him to fuck me harder. But I couldn't. I had to bite my lip and just moan it out. He must've figured out what I was moaning because he grabbed my hair and told me to "say it." I played dumb moaned "say what?".

"Tell me fuck you Gina. Say it."

Just as I open my mouth to say it, the rainbow takes over and I hear myself speak in a thousand languages. When the pretty colors in my head started to subside and I feel my heart beat again, Perry moved about 4 inches to the left and I don't know what his wand touched in there, but the spectrum came to me this time in a million colors with flecks of crystals sparkling everywhere. I thought I was going to die. Literally. I didn't think my body could handle this. This is my first multi-orgasmic experience. I think I did die. Please let me go back to earth to tell somebody I plead with St. Peter at the Pearly Gates. On my descent to earth, I look over and see Perry smiling at me. Obviously he had accompanied me to heaven, but I was so caught up in my own journey I hadn't realized it. He reached over to hold me and just then the ringing phone startled us. Brought us back to reality. The reality of what we had done. I had caused this man to sin. We looked as if we had been caught. As if the person on the other end of the phone could see us and knew what we had done. And worst of all, Perry had cussed. That was a bigger sin than sex. He'd said "fuck".

When Perry came back from taking his phone call, we both did whatever we could to avoid eye contact. I grab the comforter and wrap myself in it like the white girls on the daytime soaps do after sex, and go to the bathroom. Perry looks away as I walk pass him and pretends to be getting something from his pants pocket on the floor.

Inside the bathroom I don't know how I should feel. So I just stand there looking back at the door. I guess I should shower. Cleanliness is next to Godliness, and right now I need all the help I can get. As I turn to step in the shower, I notice a tingling on the right side of my body. It feels like ants are crawling on me. By the time I try to lift my leg to get in the shower, I can't even move it. And I feel my chest tightening. I hear Perry calling my name, but I can't answer. My tongue feels like cotton and I can't get any air. I struggle to get to the door so Perry can call for help. Then I feel something on my shoulder. It's a hand. I scream. Three seconds feel like an eternity. Then I wake up. Perry is standing over me on the sofa asking if I'm okay. I figured out that I must've fallen asleep there after he talked me out of leaving when I stormed away from the dinner table. My right arm and leg felt numb because of the position I was sleeping in. Then I remembered my dream. I pulled at my skirt and blouse, it was all still there and intact. I wonder if Perry had watched me. I wonder if he knew what I dreamt. I hope not. And lord knows I hope he didn't see me catch the rainbow. But the dream seemed so real. I looked up at Perry and sat up. He was still in his white tee and slacks. It was just a dream.

Leads to Truth

Planning a wedding is not as much fun I'd dreamed it would be. Too much to think about. Flowers, cake, dresses, fabric, vows-my head was spinning.

"Mon, can we take a break?" I begged my sister. "We've been going over this stuff for 2 hours".

"No Gina, we have to get this done. Now you really need to make a decision on flowers today so the centerpieces can be ordered on time."

"Monica, I don't care, do lilies."

"Fine Gina, Lilies. Now, did Perry give you his final decision on groomsmen? You all are really giving me a headache with this wedding. Just elope, dang."

"Yes, he gave me his four, plus Kiah. I wanted Kiah to be an honorary bridesmaid, but Perry didn't like that idea so he just made him a groomsman."

Monica stopped and just looked at me.

"What? Kiah has been through everything with me and I was not about to leave him out of my day. And besides he wants to do it."

"Okay."

"Okay? That's all you have to say?" I edge her on. I hate when she does that. She gave me that "okay", as if to say, *okay you're messing up. I'm just going to watch and then say I told you so*. Ooh she makes me sick sometimes.

"Yeah, Gina. Okay. What do you want me to say? You're a grown woman. A grown ass woman."

Fine. She doesn't have to tell me what she thinks. I know I'm making the right decision. Kiah is the truest male friend I have. I know he wants to be a part of my day. I have to be honest though, I was secretly hoping he was a little jealous. That would mean that he still cares about me. He's going to be in town this weekend. Says he has some business to take care of, but I think he's going to try to talk me out of getting married. Hell, he might ask me to marry *him* instead. So I agreed to have lunch with him on Friday, we'll see what Mr. Kiah has to say to the love of his life then. Plus, he can go and get fitted for his tux. I always thought rental tuxes were so cheap and cheesy, but Perry doesn't want a long engagement, so I'm trying to plan the wedding of the century in a month's time. Of course the word at the church is that I must be pregnant, since we are "in such a hurry". Forget them old ladies, all up in my business. Then on top of them having something to whisper every time I walk by, Perry is making me become "active" in the church. Got me teaching a Sunday school class. Gina Anniston teaching Sunday school…Now you know he done tripped and fell. I agreed to teach the 5 year olds, hell they don't know if I know what I'm talking about or not. They just want to hurry up and get through the lesson so they can color the pictures of Moses and them. And now I'm on the church Advisory Board too. I got some advice for the heifers: Stay out my business!

Headed to the Hilton Garden Inn near the airport to meet Kiah for lunch on Friday was a transportation nightmare. There was a terrible accident on I-95 and traffic was at a standstill. I only had an hour for lunch, but had planned to take 2 hours. Looks like an hour of that will be spent in traffic. I call Kiah to let him know I'm running late.

"That's cool Gina, my meeting was this morning so I'm done for today. After lunch I was going to head out to World Golf Village and get a round in."

"Well maybe I'll hang with you. Be your caddy." I joked.

"You should. You don't have to go back to work?"

"Well if you really want me to hang I can afford to take the rest of the day off. You know I'm about to marry a wealthy man. Thinking about giving the gig up altogether." Now where did that come from? I'd never even thought about that and how it managed to roll off my lips is surely a mystery to me. I guess I my subconscious wanted to draw a reaction from Kiah. He didn't buy it.

"Okay cool, call me when you get here and I'll be waiting for you in the lobby."

So here I am calling my job again to let them know I won't be returning from lunch. I didn't offer them any explanation, only instructions to please put a leave form on my desk. I didn't need anyone accusing me of "stealing" time. Especially Senora Pest, Marilyn.

Pulling up in the parking lot of the Hilton, I check my make-up and make a mental note to change my moisturizer to something heavier. Could be the changing of the seasons or maybe the stress of planning a wedding, but little dry patches are forming on my forehead and cheeks. Not cute, but too late to worry about. Since I'm not going back to work, maybe I can get Kiah to swing by the St. John's Towne Centre with me so I can make a pit stop in Sephora to buy some kind of heavy cream product.

As soon as Kiah gets into my car, he comments that he can't believe its clean seeing that it usually serves as my portable office/closet/dressing room/filing system. I tell him to f-off and once again remember that I need to quit talking like that. I'm the first lady to-be of a quite critical congregation. That thought makes me realize that I can't be seen out in public with Kiah either. There are over 5000 members in the church and I'm bound to run into one of them somewhere.

"Kiah do you mind if we eat here at the hotel? I told you about how the church ladies have been watching my every move, and the last thing I want to see Sunday morning is Sister Brown getting up doing a power point presentation with a picture of me and you as the opening slide."

"Girl them people got you tripping, huh? That's so unlike you Gina. You useta not give a care who thought whatever about you. You changing girl. You changing."

The way he said that meant it wasn't a good thing. He said it like he was disappointed. It made me feel sad that he thought that about me, but I shook it off and ignored the comment.

"So, do you mind?" I insisted.

"Fine with me, but you can only hide who you are for so long. Time will eventually walk you down."

Why are all of my so-called friends so insistent on believing that I'm such a freakin' fraud? None of them have taken the time so see if I've really changed or not. And am I really that bad of a person that I have to become someone totally different now to be accepted by the "church people"? I think these *friends* are the ones with the problem. They are afraid that if I do happen to change they will be the "worse" apple in the crew. Everybody wants to have Gina in their life so they won't feel so bad when they cuss, or drink too much, or hell, sleep with somebody just for g.p. - general purposes. And why does Kiah care anyway? He needs quit worrying about me and start worrying about that chicken head he rolled up to my party with a few months ago.

Inside the hotel restaurant my paranoia sets in again. I start to think what if one of the servers is church member. They'll think I'm staying here with Kiah. It's like I can't escape this whole preacher's wife thing. This is not going to be an easy ride. I decide to relax and set my mind elsewhere, not worry about it. I have colleagues, family, and friends. And if these so-called Christians want to judge me, they need to read in the bible: *Judge not, that you be not judged.*

Lunch was good. I had crab cakes and pasta with butter sauce. Forgot all about trying to fit into my "off the rack" wedding dress. Whatever. Since it's off the rack I can just go up a size. I take that back, I already have to get a size 14, if I have to get a 16, I will officially be considered one of the real "plus size" girls. Hell to the nawl. Not ready to admit that. Did I say "hell to the nawl"? I gotta quit watching "Being Bobby Brown". That darn Whitney is off the heazy. Kiah had baby back ribs and veggies. And he was sucking on those bones like he was hungry too. I mean *hungry.* During lunch he tried to talk me into going to World Golf Village with him to meet his boy. He really thought I would caddy for him. He must be crazy. The only kind of bag I'm dragging today is shaped like a square and has two paper handles on it. I'm going shopping just like I planned. Maybe I'll ride out to the village with him though. They have a few shops out there and its nice weather so it'll be nice to get out.

I went up to Kiah's room with him- ducking and dodging the whole way, of course- so he could change into his "lucky" golf shirt. He is so lame for that. I sat on the bed while he took his shirt off and put the other one on. I pretended not to notice his six pack abs. That negro is like a fine wine. I swear he looks better and better as he gets older.

"That is the ugliest shade of green I have ever seen" I said to him.

"That's money green, girl. You don't know nothing bout that. That's grown folks style there."

"Hmph. Whatever you say. Let's go."

"Nah, it's early. I'm supposed to meet him at 4:30. We got an hour to chill, you want to watch Maury?"

"No, I don't watch that stupid mess. It's like he does the same story everyday. We already know the paternity test is going to reveal that the baby is not the dude's. Who really buys into that stuff? You can watch it; I'll play solitaire on your laptop."

"Yeah, you can play on my laptop anytime girl. Right here." He said pointing at his lap. He's so silly.

I shot him a bird and set his laptop up to play. I rolled my eyes every time he burst out laughing at that stupid show. I don't understand how someone who is as intelligent as he is can be entertained by such stupidity.

Leaving the hotel at 6pm that evening I can't believe I'd fallen asleep for that long. But more than that, I can't believe I'd betrayed my husband to-be. I'd done it by sleeping with Kiah. I cannot believe I let that happen. I don't even know how it happened.

All I know is that I was sitting there playing freaking solitaire and the next thing I know Kiah was in my face with those almond eyes telling me to quit being scared. I resisted with my mouth but my feet and body moved freely to the place he was trying to take me. I tried to wake, hoping I'd fallen asleep at the computer, but this was no dream. This time I was wide awake. The pain in my side and the lump in my throat told me this was the real thing. It's like I just forgot all about my new life and fell into my old ways for a moment of pleasure. I can't even really say it was for pleasure. More so to prove a point to myself. I was so hurt when Kiah showed up to my party with another woman, that even though that was months ago and I'm sure the heifer has not thought about me once, I figured I would be proving to her that he was mine. Even though she'll probably never know about this little episode, I felt I owed myself that much. And more than that, I had to prove to myself that he still wanted me. That he still loved me. Dang. Did I say love?

Soul Redemption

So here I am on my wedding day. The church is beautiful. Monica did a great job with overseeing the décor. White Calla lilies line the aisles and the altar of the church. I don't know if I'll ever get to see heaven, but if I do I imagine that this is what it smell and look like. I'd always dreamed of roses on my wedding day. But somehow, it just didn't seem fitting for Perry and I. So lilies it was. I would be the only rose in the church today. Battered, tattered, and torn. But still a rose.

I'd decided on an early afternoon wedding, so the light shining in the stained glass windows gave off a warm glow that just looks like…well, looks like love. My bridesmaids were due to arrive any moment, but while I had the whole church to myself I decided that this was as good a time as any to have a much needed talk with God. I know it was a fine time to be asking Her to show me if I was doing the right thing, but never the less I pleaded for Her to give me a sign. Before I finished my prayer, I heard squealing behind me. My girls had arrived. Sharon, Serena, Monica, and two of my other close friends from high school, Marla and Dana. Dana was living in Japan with her military husband, and had come halfway around the world for my day. I felt like the luckiest woman in the world. We instinctively went into a group hug, all pressed face to face to face.

"It is so gorgeous in here," Dana said while looking up into the high ceilings, "I can't wait to meet Perry. He must be a heck of a man to tame Ms. Gina."

"I know right," added Serena, "I thought my girl was gon' be a playa for life, hear me?"

"Come on, yall," I chided, "It's my wedding day, cut a sister a break."

"You know we just teasing with you girl. I'm so happy for you. Gina, you deserve all of this and so much more." Serena actually sounded sincere.

"Um, Gina," Sharon cut in, "I know we're having a sappy moment right now and everything but I need to clear this up before we go anotha furtha. I know Perry is a preacher and all, but err ahh, are we gon' have some liquor up in the reception?"
Everybody burst into laughter, but I know Sharon was dead serious.

"I got you covered Sharon. We're having champagne."

"Cristal?"

"Don't push it Share. Come on yall; let me show you where we'll be getting dressed."

We walked down the long corridor to the Christian Education classroom that Monica had transformed into a dressing room. She'd thought of everything. There were 6 dressing areas in the large room. Each had a vanity table with a mirror and chair. There were fresh cut flowers, full length mirrors, a table with snacks and sparkling water. I mean my sister had gone all out. There was soft music playing. In my dressing area were framed pictures of me and my sister and brother when we were younger and one of Perry and I-the one we'd put in the Florida Times-Union Newspaper for our engagement announcement. The moment took over. The tears started to flow. Monica brought me Kleenex and asked if I was okay.

"Just happy. And wishing he were here to see this." I said motioning at the picture of my brother in his green and white soccer shorts and flip flops.

"I know. But he's watching. From up there," She said pointing upwards.

That made me feel a little better. I took a sip of my water and looked at my watch. Quarter after eleven. I'd be making my entrance to my new life in less than two hours. I looked at the white and gold Teeleman's Bridal dress bag and decided I wasn't ready to get dressed yet. I walked back out into the church area and someone yelled "Bride's coming", the signal to remove Perry from the vestibule so he couldn't see me.

"Don't worry, not in my dress yet," I yelled.

"Don't matter. He shouldn't see you." Somebody yelled back.

I never believed in bad luck. Now bad karma, that was something to believe in. What you put out there will come back to you eventually. Like Kiah said, time will walk you down. The way I had been living, I wasn't waiting for time to walk me down, it's like I'd been chasing time; walking it down. I walked through the foyer of the church and peeped in the sanctuary one last time. It didn't even look like something that could be for me. It was too pristine. This looked like the preparation of a ceremony for someone who'd lived a life deserving of this. Certainly not me. Maybe my sister Monica, who'd opted for a courthouse wedding, maybe even Sharon, but not me. I took a deep breath, and went back to the C.E. room to get dressed.

"Might as well get my hat and cane and get on with the show." I said out loud to no one in particular.

"Might as well." A voice came from behind me. I swung around not believing I'd heard I thought I'd heard. It was Sean.

"What are you doing he.. I mean, how did you know I was getting married?"

"Saw it in the paper. My homeboy's girl saw it and called him. You know how the grapevine goes. Anyway…I'm here."

"Well you look nice in your suit. I'm glad you came."

"Yeah I came early hoping for a private moment with you. I want to apologize for.."

"No need," I cut in. "All is forgiven."

With that, I turned and entered the room to put on my dress and white veil. Funny though, I've always worn a veil. Just nobody knew it was there but me. All people ever saw was my million dollar smile. They never knew that, like Paul Lawrence Dunbar, I wore the mask that grinned and lied. Grinned to hide the pain of constant rejection, of seeking love outside of myself, and most of all, of ignoring the voice of God. But in this moment I've decided that when Perry lifts that veil from my face, all things old will become new again. I thought about what I'd said to Sean 'All is forgiven'. It was that easy. God spoke to me in that moment. The answer I'd been asking Her for came in an instant. No fanfare, no shouting, no passing out on the floor. Just a quiet moment alone with God, and I became a new person.

Butterfly Karma

Walking down that aisle seemed like the longest walk of my life. To my left were the faces of friends from near and far, old and new. To my right were mostly people I didn't know. Some of them looked slightly familiar, with facial features similar to Perry's. Those must have been his aunts and uncles. There were children smiling and pointing at me. I saw lots of church members. Some of them looked genuinely happy to be there. Others looked as if they just came to see what they could see. The church was packed. I held my Dad's arm so tight that I'm sure it was cutting off his circulation. He didn't let on though. As I neared the front, I saw my mother take her lace handkerchief from her champagne colored purse and dab her eyes. I started to mist up a little myself. My girls were looking like 5 black Barbie dolls in their sage green silk dresses. Monica was crying and Sharon was nudging her trying to make her stop. I had to chuckle at Sharon's obliviousness that everyone could see her doing that. Still clueless as ever.

My eyes finally met Perry's. He looked like the happiest man in the world. Outsiders probably couldn't tell he was nervous. But I know him, I could see it in his eyes. He had that faraway look in his eyes. He was smiling at me, but his eyes said his thoughts were going a mile a minute. His breathing even looked a little labored, but so was mine. When I finally got to him and my father kissed my cheek and figuratively and literally gave me away, I felt a relief. All the people that said Gina and Perry wouldn't make it to the altar had to sit in their seats and witness me marry my man. The preacher man.

My eyes went to Kiah; he was looking out into the congregation. Wouldn't even make eye contact with me. I needed him to give me a glance of approval, but he wouldn't even look at me. For a fleeting moment, I wished it was him holding my hand. I wished he was my groom, and I knew that all the reservations I was having about getting married wouldn't even be an issue. Perry caught my eyes searching for Kiah's approval and I looked away, then back at Perry. I tried listening to the preacher say whatever it was he was saying, but it all became one big blur. What I heard was God speaking to me again. The gold tooth I saw flashing from the corner of the preachers mouth was proof that he was talking, but his voice was not what I was hearing. I heard God asking me if I believed the Son was sent to the cross to die so that I might live.

"I do" I replied.

God then ask me if I agreed to serve Her for the rest of my days and spread the gospel to non-believers.

"I do," I said again. And as I said it, it looked as if Kiah was mouthing the words with me. Was he saying I do to me, or was God speaking to him as well? I had to believe God was talking to him too.

I came back to reality and heard the preacher say "… the rings please."

I turned to Sharon and she handed me the plain gold band that Perry had chosen. He said that he was a simple man and did not want to be too flashy. When I turned back around with the ring, I realized that Perry had forgotten to give his best man the ring before the ceremony. I knew I should have reminded him. Perry reached into his own pocket to get the ring and I hoped not too many people noticed the oversight. Every bride wants her day to be perfect. As he brought the ring from his pocket, he didn't hand it to the preacher as the preacher had asked. He turned directly to me with it. Then I noticed it wasn't the ring I had chosen. It was a silver ring. The silver ringed barrel of a gun.

  The church filled with shrieks and screams and people scrambling for the door. I saw Kiah and the other groomsmen moving toward Perry and my bridesmaids scrambling up through the pulpit toward the side entrance. The door Perry enters every Sunday morning to do his sermon. Everything was happening so fast, but I was seeing things in slow motion. Perry looked like he was sick. His eyes were half closed and his mouth opened as if he were going to vomit. He aimed the silver pistol at me and as my body reacted by diving to the ground I saw a rainbow. This time it wasn't a pretty rainbow. Fire orange with a flash of blue is what I saw. I felt a hot sensation in my side and felt like I was lying in a pool of warm water. That was the first shot. I guess Perry saw that I wasn't dead and was going for the kill because I heard another shot, and then another. By then I was blacking out. I looked up to see my mother passed out near me and my father and sister standing over me screaming. Then darkness.

Truth Equals Light

144

I woke up to a white light and a sore throat. I must not be dead because I would not be feeling pain. I heard hard quick footsteps. It was my mother rushing to my bed, which meant I must be in a hospital. I tried to speak but no words came from my mouth. I panicked and tried to get up. My mother held me down and told me to calm down, that I would be okay. I gave her a helpless expression. I wanted to know what had happened. Then I remembered something about a white dress. It was my wedding day. My husband had shot me. I felt my chest tighten and heard a series of quick beeps. I tried to put my hand to my chest but there were tubes everywhere. The one in my mouth kept me from speaking. Nurses ran in and pumped fluid in and out of me. Adjusted machinery, and gave me a shot of something. I heard, between dozing in and out of consciousness, a nurse tell my mom to tell me as little as possible about what happened until they could get me more stabilized.

After about two nights in what must have been the ICU, they finally removed the tubes and gave me a sip of water. I was told I would be moved from the trauma unit to a regular room. I still had no clue as to why Perry shot me and if he'd been arrested or what. Nobody told me anything, and I couldn't stay awake long enough to overhear enough conversations, nor to be mentally distressed about the events. For days, all I remember is waking up and looking at a pale green curtain, a nurse looking at something on the side of my bed, and my mom, dad, and sister sitting around not saying much of anything. If I hadn't been so doped up, I imagine

I might have gone mad. Maybe I had gone mad, but I was too drugged to really worry about it now.

After sleeping again for what may have been a couple of hours, or days-I couldn't really tell, I woke up for the first time and felt almost coherent. My mom was there and immediately stood and came to my side. White Linen. She always wore too much perfume but this was one time I was happy to be smelling it.

"Hi sleepy-head."

It took me a minute to get a sound to come out of my mouth. Finally I got a breath big enough to produce a whisper.

"Did they get him?" I was talking about Perry. Were they even looking for him? Just thinking about it made me upset. Mama reached down to my side a pressed a thing that looked like those buzzer buttons on Jeopardy. I saw a clear fluid slowly going through one of the tubes attached somewhere to me.

"You just rest baby. You are safe here."

Why were they keeping me so drugged? I felt myself panicking at the thought of sleeping for 2 or 3 more days and begin ripping tubes from my arm.

"No Gina calm down baby its okay. No, you need this medicine. It'll help you feel better."

By then I guess she'd pressed the button for a nurse because a lady wearing a bright pink smock and matching pants came running in. She grabbed me to hold me down and called for help on the speaker.

"Leave me alone! I don't need this I'm not sick-get off me." I feel a burning sensation in my arm and all the way down one side of my body. Somehow I guess they must've given me a shot of some of that liquid cocaine they had me on because I felt a rush of calm come over my body. While the team of nurses hooked up another thousand tubes and crap to me, a man in a pale yellow short sleeved dress shirt and some wrinkled khakis came and stood beside me. He peered down over me with his rimless glasses and all I could see was his nose hairs. He looked closer and then turned to my mother as if I wasn't there and asked if I was awake. Hello asshole, don't you see my eyes open, I thought.

"Yes I'm awake, do you not see me?" I was aggravated and why does he want to know my business anyway. He must be a pitiful ass excuse for a doctor; he didn't even have a stethoscope. He ignored me.

My mom did too and answered him, "Yes, she's coherent enough to understand".

Dr. Wrinkled Pants sat down in the vinyl green chair-what is it with hospitals and the color green? Get a clue; I thought the color of blue water was supposed to be the healing color. They must want to keep people sick so they can tap the hell out of insurance companies. Insurance, oh God, my job. I forgot I had a job. Maybe I don't anymore.

"Gina I'm Bill and I work here at the hospital as a counselor. I counsel people through post traumatic therapy," he started. "Do you know what happened to you?"

I looked at my mother who gave me a look that said it was okay and then looked back at wrinkled pants-I mean Bill.

"Yes, I was going to get married and he tried to kill me, I think." The reality of talking about caused whatever that machine was beeping to speed up and my mom stood and came to my side.

"It's okay Gina," she said. "We'll just talk about it a little at a time. Yes, Perry shot you but the important thing is that you made it. We don't know why he did it but you made it."

Over the next couple of days the nurses and doctors explained to me that I had been shot in the side and the bullet made a clean exit wound only damaging a part of my large intestine, which had been removed during a surgery. They removed the catheter, which I didn't realize I had until about day 2 or 3 of wondering why I didn't have to pee. Between nurses changing bandages and adding and removing tubes, Bill would come in with my mom and dad and tell me little bits of what happened on the day I was shot. Some days I wished Perry hadn't missed. I was miserable. Here I am thinking I'm the luckiest woman in the world one day, and the next day I'm laying in a sterile smelling hospital having people wipe my mouth and ass for me.

"I have a surprise for you." Bill told me on this particular day. In walked Sharon and Monica. For the first time in the 4 or 5 days or weeks I'd been here, I smiled. Or at least I think I did. I don't know whether my face was messed up or not. Probably was. Nobody had offered to show me a mirror during my brief waking periods when they allowed me to get off the liquid crack long enough to talk to mom and Dr. Bill.

"Hey girl!" Sharon said too loud and everyone looked at her as if to give her a clue that I was crazy and yelling might upset me. She took the hint and lowered her voice. "I'm glad you're alright, you scared me."

"Me too, sis," that was Monica. "I'm so glad to see you awake and talking. You don't know how glad I am."

"I'm glad to see yall too," I said. "They don't let me stay awake long enough to ask about you guys. Is everybody okay? What are people saying?"

Dr. Bill cut in. "Gina, they want to talk about you. They've been waiting to see you and we can only let them stay a few minutes."

I was not talking to him and I didn't even look at him. They messed up today by not giving me my crack medicine because I was more coherent than ever. I kept my eyes on Sharon and Monica and asked again, "How is everybody?"

They avoided eye contact with me and looked at Dr. Bill and then my mom. Mama looked at Bill and walked over to him. After a brief moment, Bill turns and walks out of the room motioning for Monica and Sharon to follow him. They do. Then Mom comes over and smiles at me as she wants me to smile back. I don't.

"Gina, I don't want to keep things from you. Perry shot Kiah too." I try to cut in but she doesn't let me. "Kiah didn't make it, baby."

Every bit of air and life I have in my body escapes me. I let out a sound that I didn't know I had the strength in me to make.

Mama didn't flinch other than to wrap both her arms around my shoulders and pull her body close to me. She rocked, and then continued. "Then he turned the gun on himself. He's dead too." She picked up the Jeopardy buzzer medicine thingy and continued to rock me as she pressed the button as hard as she could. This time I didn't resist the medication. I put my hand on top of hers and helped her press the button harder. I felt myself slipping into oblivion. In my mind the events from the wedding day played in my head as the room got fuzzier and quieter. I heard 3 shots rang out again. I remember thinking all 3 were for me. I wish they had been. Blackness.

New Beginnings

Leaving my little corner of the sky apartment that day felt funny. Knowing that wouldn't return to this place as home made me feel kind of sad. Sad like I felt the day they buried Kiah. My therapists and doctors had refused to give me medical clearance to attend the funeral, so that day I just lay in my hospital bed and watched the clouds through the small vertical window. I'd envisioned Kiah ascending the steps of heaven with his familiar black leather coat and Timberland boots on. I don't know why I felt like that's what he was wearing, but I did. I knew it was my fault Kiah was dead, but in the same breath, I believed I'd seen Kiah say "I do" to God on what was supposed to be my wedding day, so I feel relieved that at least he made it into the Kingdom. Nevertheless I felt like I had pulled the trigger. In a sense, I had. Perry found out that I had slept with Kiah the weekend he was in town on business. On the morning of our wedding, someone delivered a type-written letter with details of that day, along with pictures of Kiah and I at lunch, and of me leaving the hotel that evening. No one has yet to come forward with information on who delivered the package. At this point it doesn't matter. Kiah is gone, and so is Perry. It's been six months since the incident and it still feels like yesterday. I keep wishing I could go back in time and change my own tire that day. I should have let Perry keep driving.

Once I had the last box of my personal things in my car, I went back upstairs to make sure the movers hadn't forgotten anything. Moving back home to Georgia to start over was not something I had made peace with easily. I knew I had to get out of Jacksonville though; my face and Perry's face had been on too many news broadcasts and newspapers since the incident. I tried not to watch the news, I quit my job, I avoided crowds, but I still could not avoid the madness. Everywhere I went people whispered and nudged one another. I felt like a circus freak some days, and other days I ignored the stares and gasps and went on about my business.

On my last glance of the apartment I noticed that I'd left my two potted plants on the balcony. They were both basically dead so there was no use taking them with me. One was a miniature rose bush that Kiah had given me the day he came to be fitted for his tux. In the past, he'd always given me orchids because he knew they were my favorite. But that particular time he'd given me roses. I looked at the miniature bush with so much pain in my heart. On one of the stems was a tiny pink bud sprouting. I picked up the plant and took a breath as I descended the stairs.

Acknowledgments

Thank you God for the gift. Many have it, some recognize it, few use it. Thank you for allowing me to be one of the chosen few.

Mama, what can I say? You have been more than a mother, a friend, and a confidante. Your smile is my sunshine. You are truly my everything. Thank you for believing in me.

To my muses, Leila, Gabby, Dee-Dee, and Desmond; thank you for lifting my writer's block. You guys give me endless hope…and laughter. And yes Leila, "Desmond did it."

Wendy, you are everything a girl could ask for in a sister. You are amazing. Thank you for allowing me to be your shadow.

Nicole, your work inspires me. Keep on pushing sister! Greatness is at your fingertips.

Mecca, Thank you for telling me the truth, whether I like it or not.

My freshman year roommate Keisha E.; thank you for being the first person to tell me my work didn't belong in a closet. Where are you? Miss you!

Grandma and Grandpa; thank you for holding the family together. You guys are the epitome of what a family should be. I love you both.

What up Bryan! Big things await you my brother, trust me.

There are countless others who have touched my life, my soul, my imagination to make it possible to put my creativity on paper. You know who you are; Thank you.

Daddy, I miss you. Rest in Peace. Till we meet again…

About the Author

Lisa Webb Timley is a native of Albany, Georgia. She received her Bachelor of Arts degree in Mass Communications at Savannah State University, and is seeking her Masters of Education Technology from Jacksonville University. Aside from being a writer, she is an educator in Jacksonville, Florida. She is currently working on her second novel *Getting Over*.

www.ingramcontent.com/pod-product-compliance
Lightning Source LLC
Chambersburg PA
CBHW031605260626
47154CB00020B/1621